Mis*Adventures

~ The Great

Jungle ~

Mis*Adventures

~ The Great

Jungle ~

by Lakesha Brown

Book Cover by Lakesha Brown

[979-8-9908140-1-1] edition 2024

Table of Contents

Prologue

Steven Logan was on top of the world at a young age, and

he led the world into a new era of medical science with his

discoveries in medicine and technology. Steven's company,

Lotus Incorporated, created a cure that could reverse the

stages of cancer in a person's body regardless of how late

the doctors found it. Steven also made better-cost-effected

devices for physical and mental disabilities, such as

affordable in-home therapy equipment. Steven Logan

became a household name after his accomplishments,

especially with his motto, "We all should aim to be the best

versions of ourselves. This way, society will advance in a

positive way!"

Steven took another step in trying to make the world a better place by founding his school. Steven created Silver Valley High School in Silver Valley, Colorado, United States of America. The school became well-known throughout the world. It has the highest cost of admission for a high school globally, but it is known to have the best facilities of any current educational program. Rumors spread that Steven was planning to open a college in a few years, but he denounced the rumors faster than they could be created.

He shared his life with his two adoptive daughters, whom he was lucky enough to know when they were babies. Steven had known their parents for years until their accident. After their deaths, he took on himself to look after the girls. He shielded his two daughters from the spotlight. A few people knew their appearance, and even fewer knew about their situation.

The only way a person outside the selective few that Steven allowed into his inner circle. If they were in, then they had access to his home office. Inside his office, in a

cabinet on the right side of the wall, Steven hid a collection

of books he had acquired during his young adult days.

Even if the public had access to this information, no

one would believe it, as Steven looked completely different

from the people shown in the books. He was a white man

with blond hair with hints of grey. Steven looked older for

his age, but people chalked it up as him once being very ill.

There has been a long-time rumor that Steven is a former

cancer patient, but he never confirmed whether it was true.

However, this rumor gained him sympathy from the public.

Steven was the ideal type of human. Excluding the

money, his family was like everyone else, or at least what

families wanted to be. If only his family thought the same

thing.

Chapter 1

Ordinary

In a high school history classroom, Jazmine closed a video from her phone that was a five-minute summary of the documentary that the teacher was showing about her father. It was the fifth class that semester to play a documentary about him. She sighed and opened an old book that she found in his study. It was one of many journals from the room that she had been reading for a year. She remembered stories from when the family's butler told her and her sister bedtime stories. He never read the books directly, but they were almost identical when he told the story. The only difference that Jazmine could tell was that he told the story from a different point of view.

Before reading, Jazmine looked up at the clock next to the door. There were less than ten minutes left in class. Jazmine flipped to the last entry that she had read.

July XX

We believe that we found another portal in the mountains. I don't know how he does it, but he manages to find one every time. It looks like no one lives near the area, so we should have an easier time getting to the next world. I hope we can explore it this time and draw some nice pictures. I'm happy as long as it is warmer than the last world.

There were still three minutes left after reading the short entry. Jazmine carefully returned the book to her bag. She leaned back in her desk and counted the many spots on the ceiling tile. It was the week before winter break. This meant that teachers would give their students busy work and not have to deal with them. Surprised that the teacher did not provide them with a coloring sheet, Jazmine did not see the point of her being at school. It was the same thing every day. She sighed as she looked back down at the documentary that was playing. The only person who was paying attention to the video was her sister.

Alexandra was busy jotting down facts that came from the documentary. Unlike her sister, Alexandra was happy with her life. There was nothing to complain about. She went to the best school in the country, already had a full ride to any college of her choice with three and a half years of high school left and would never have to worry about money for the rest of her life. She only broke out of focus when the bell rang.

Most people, including the teacher, rushed out the door. Alexandra checked her watch before packing her things away. She said something to herself that Jazmine could not hear from her desk. Jazmine laid her head down. Even though she was ready to leave, she did not want to stand up. She would wait until Alexandra came to get her. Before that could happen, one of Jazmine's friends, Davis, walked into the classroom.

Davis greeted everyone as he walked past them and dropped his bag next to Jazmine. He had already loosened his school tie even though the dismissal bell had just rung.

"I thought today would never end," Jazmine groaned.

"Awe, Jazzy, we got one more day to go through. Don't you draw during class anyway?" he joked as he played with one of Jazmine's locks.

Jazmine swatted Davis's hand away. "Don't touch the hair, Davis."

She knew Davis wished he had his hair styled like hers. He could not get his hair done like this because his mother had forbidden it. From what Davis had told her, his mom believed he looked better with a fade. Jazmine had recommended he wear a wig from the drama club if he wanted to try the hair out, but Davis refused.

Davis laughed and sat down next to Jazmine. He pulled out his phone. After a couple of swipes, the article appeared. It was from the school's news website: Silver Valley Chronicles. The beginning of the report showed a picture of two teenagers their age. The two of them seemed to be twins because of their similar features. The only difference was that one had blue highlights in their hair. It was hard for Jazmine to figure out which twin was the male and the other female.

"Looks like we're getting a pair of new students next semester. Recognize them?" Davis asked.

"Never met them in person, but those are the Bellini twins. Their family is old money that has been passed down for generations. Mrs. Bellini died a couple of years ago because of cancer," Jazmine answered.

"Cancer? You'd think rich people like them would buy one of your dad's products?"

"I guess not everyone believes in science."

Davis shrugged and flipped through his phone for more articles. Before he could pull up another report, Alexandra walked up in front of them, along with her friend, Ji-yoon. Alexandra had exceptionally long hair tied into a low ponytail. She had a notepad and red glitter pen in her hand. While she had dark skin, it was lighter than Jazmine's or Davis's. As the tallest girl in their grade, Alexandra made herself taller by wearing platform shoes.

Ji-yoon did not pay much attention to what was happening around her, she was too busy scrolling through her phone. The yellow phone case she used matched perfectly with her nails. Unlike Alexandra, Ji-yoon had short, curly black hair and wore makeup highlighting her tan skin tone.

Alexandra and Ji-yoon had matching patches on their uniforms. The patches meant the two were part of the school's life maintenance club. The club aimed to make chosen students watch and correct other students to keep order. The members of the life maintenance club had different uniforms than the rest of the student body. Since it was winter, regular students wore blue

uniforms that included a blazer or cardigan, dress shoes, and

pants or skirts, depending on the student's preference. Alexandra

and Ji-yoon's uniforms were black, as the uniforms matched other

life maintenance club members' outfits. Ji-yoon wore the school's

cardigan instead of the blazer. She claimed it's more comfortable

for her.

"Davis, you didn't put your tie on properly," Alexandra

scolded. She straightened his tie before he could do it himself and

then scanned him to find any other problems with his appearance.

"School is technically out, so it doesn't matter," he pointed

out.

"But you're still on school grounds. Plus, as a student of

Silver Valley Academy, you should always have pride in your

appearance," Alexandra warned. "If I catch you again like this, I

will be forced to write you up."

Davis rolled his eyes. "Fine."

"I see you two are reading the school's news. What do you

think about my column?" Ji-yoon asked.

"Honestly, I don't know what's more amazing. Your

ability to find information about everything that goes on around here, Ji-yoon, or Jazzy's ability to know everyone without meeting them first," Davis said.

"I don't know everyone. My father just forces us to learn about every wealthy person's life," Jazmine complained. "There's no reason for it."

"Of course, there is Jazmine!" Alexandra exclaimed. "If we don't know them, how do you expect us to take over the family business?"

"How are we supposed to take over the company if it doesn't let us meet these important people?" Jazmine said. Then she thought, "he keeps us in the dark about everything."

"Now, come on, you two agreed to help us with our inspection this week," Alexandra said.

Jazmine and Davis groaned but got up. This was the only way that the two of them could stay after school. It was against the rules for students to be on school grounds after school hours unless it was for tutoring or a club activity. Even students who lived in dorms weren't allowed to be in the facilities during off-hours. Davis and Jazmine's after-school activities were on Mondays, Wednesdays, and Fridays. However, their clubs were done until the spring.

"This place is too big," Jazmine thought as she looked out the window to see parts of the school ground.

The school was divided into five sections. The most prominent building on the property was the classroom building to the East. Students spent most of their time here. The floor levels were divided into class years, with the first-year students working on the first floor and the seniors on the fourth. The roof was accessible for students, but no one went up there during the winter.

North of the classroom was the library. The United Library Board voted the Silver Valley library highly in the best libraries in the world poll. This is because it also doubled as a museum that changed every season to allow students to learn more about the history of other countries. The information given at the library was not just for essays but also for curious minds.

On the West side of campus, the teachers' facility was located. Even though each floor of the student building had multiple rooms for the teachers to work in, they made a separate building to give teachers time for themselves. It was not as big as the other building but closer to the entrance. This allowed teachers to survey the students as they walked in and out of the property.

The sports and art faculties were close to the teachers' building. The facility caters to both outdoor and indoor sports with multiple buildings and fields. The creative program was split into three sections: music, theater, and the arts. It allowed students to make music using instruments, singing, or producing. Different art mediums, such as painting or writing, were used and welcomed. Most students joined one club offered just for the experience given.

Jazmine believed that creative writing should be added to the program, but the school considered it something students could do on their own time.

In the middle of the buildings lay the principal's office. It was nowhere near as large as any other building on the property. The principal, Steven Logan, rarely used it, as he was always off somewhere.

"I bet janitors make a killing cleaning this place," Jazmine joked in a low volume so only Davis could hear her.

"Or they're killing themselves because they have to clean this place," Davis whispered.

It was typical for the life maintenance club to solve any problem around the school, as Steven believed the students should be able to come to a conclusion about their problems. In desperate cases, teachers would involve themselves.

Alexandra took the lead in their walk around the school. She was the only one taking the job seriously. Jazmine and Davis were in the center of the group. They used this time to catch up on each other's lives. However, it seemed like Jazmine and Davis were doing more of the talking. Ji-yoon was in the back with her notebook open. While she was a part of the life maintenance club, she instead used this time to find out the latest gossip for the school's newspaper.

Nothing seemed out of the ordinary. Students were doing their club activities or leaving through the front gate. The students leaving were getting into cars or walking on foot toward the dorms. The dorms were about a mile away. It takes some students longer to walk to school since it is on a hill. The residential area home to the rest of the students was farther down the road.

"Seems like all is in order," Alexandra commented.

"Of course it is," Davis replied. "Everyone is too tired from the exams."

"Yes, there are even people who've been skipping their clubs to go home early," Ji-yoon pointed out.

"Skipping out on your activities for such a reason won't help them get into a good college," Alexandra scolded.

"Can't blame them for wanting a life outside this place," Jazmine mumbled. "Plus, if you go here, you're automatically going to a great college. The name of the school itself is good enough."

"But wouldn't you rather earn your place instead of it being given to you? We all should aim to be the best versions of ourselves. This way, society will advance in a positive way!" Alexandra exclaimed.

"You sound just like Dad," Jazmine whined.

"And it seems like you can never be bothered by anything," Alexandra snapped before realizing how loud she was being. She coughed in her hand to act as if she never raised her voice.

"Well, out of everyone in the world, the leading man in science would be a great person to be compared to," Ji-yoon pointed out.

"Thank you."

"If I didn't know the two of you, I wouldn't believe that you guys were sisters," Davis laughed.

"I have an idea. After the patrol, why don't we all head to mine and Alex's house? If you two have nothing to do?"

"I'm down. I have to get home before seven though," Davis answered.

"Sure. It's not like we do anything else."

The rest of the patrol was relatively uneventful. As Ji-yoon said, most students who had school activities had already left the school grounds. This caused their usual two-hour patrol to become only one hour. The patrol could have been shorter, but Alexandra wanted to ensure everything was in order. As they left the entrance, an older man was waiting for them in front of a small limo. He was rather attractive with his neatly combed salt and pepper hair. There were some parents picking up their children who tried to speak with him, but the man ignored them or pointed out how they wore a wedding ring. This caused the parents to run back to their cars.

"Afternoon, Mr. Ngo!" Davis greeted.

Ngo slowly closed his eyes and sighed. He opened the door to the limo to let them inside. Jazmine gave Ngo a playful salute before climbing in. Alexandra waved at Ngo before sliding

next to her sister. Ji-yoon gave a slight bow before taking her

place next to Alexandra. Davis hopped in soon after. Before

closing the door, Ngo greeted Davis back.

"Afternoon, Master Brown."

The twins' family mansion was close to the school. Steven

built the estate on one of the many mountains surrounding Silver

Valley High School. It was possible to see the entire school from

the mansion. The mansion itself was well-built. It did not seem

out of place with the surrounding environment while still looking

modern.

Ngo pulled up to the front of the mansion. He got out first

to open the door for the others. They got out one by one. As

Davis jogged up to the front door, Ji-yoon took her time. Ngo

turned his attention toward Alexandra and Jazmine before they

could follow their friends.

"I am sorry to inform you that Master Logan has already

left for a business trip overseas. He said he would be back before

the school year ends," he informed.

"But he said that we would spend Christmas together this

year," Alexandra complained.

"I know, Mistress Gomez. He sends his apologies."

"He always sends his apologies. He could have called us at least before making those types of decisions," Jazmine said. "He doesn't even pick up his phone when he's gone."

"I am sorry. I wish the two of you would also have a consistent parental figure," Ngo said. When Ngo said this, he did not try to hide his emotions like he usually did. His face looked like a mixture of sadness and annoyance.

"It's not your fault," Alexandra sighed.

"If he did anything different, it would have been the end of the world," Jazmine added. Alexandra elbowed her for saying that about their father.

"Hurry up, you two!" Davis yelled.

"Coming!" Alexandra answered.

Alexandra ran up the steps, with Jazmine just a little behind. Jazmine led them toward the game room. Before going in, Ji-yoon grabbed one of the everyday outfits that she had for when school was over. Davis could have changed out of his uniform with the random clothing he accidentally left over too, but he decided against it. Instead, he removed his blazer, which revealed a black pop-rock band shirt. He tied his blazer around his waist and his tie around his wrist so he would not forget them.

When Ji-yoon came into the room, everyone was doing something different. Looking through a red folder full of paper, Alexandra seemed frustrated at the work she needed to do. Jazmine was busy looking through an old book that Ji-yoon had seen her with before. She was sure she had seen Jazmine reading a similar book multiple times. Ji-yoon took her place between Alexandra and Jazmine.

Davis was flipping through the television channels to find something to watch. When he found nothing interesting, he put it on a random music channel. He set the remote on the table and turned his attention to the ladies. "So, what are you guys doing for winter break?"

"The same thing, as usual, I'm afraid," Alexandra answered as Jazmine nodded in agreement.

"Figured as much. But what about you, Ji-yoon? Any plans to head back to Korea for the break, and if you do, can you bring me back a souvenir?"

"No and no," she answered dryly. "I'm just going to send presents for my family through the mail and call it a day."

"Well, the three of you are no fun, as expected," Davis said. "If y'all want, you can celebrate Christmas with my mom and me. You know how she overcooks on holidays. And since we don't have any family in the area, it would be a shame to have all that food go to waste."

"Her double chocolate fudge brownies sound delicious right about now," Jazmine commented.

"Are you going to make those mango floats again?" Alexandra asked.

"Aren't you supposed to be on a diet?" Ji-yoon questioned.

"Well, mangos are healthy," Jazmine chimed in.

"Yeah, what she said," Alexandra said.

"I can always ask her, but she probably will. I just need to go to the store to get the mangoes for her, but sure."

"Don't see any reason for us not to go," Jazmine said.

"But we would have to ask Ngo if we can go first," Alexandra said.

Davis laughed. "Of course, Ngo is going to say yes. He can even come if he wants to. I already know that he's been waiting for an invitation!"

"I don't think that you understand your relationship with him," Ji-yoon mumbled.

"What do you mean?" Davis asked.

"Never mind."

Ji-yoon grabbed the remote to change the channel to the World News Channel. There was usually little action in the town, so watching the local news was pointless unless you needed to know the weather for that day. It was currently talking about the new enrollments that were happening in Silver Valley High School. The report explained how students from various parts of the world try to enlist in a better life for their families back home. Ji-yoon quickly tuned out the rest of the newscast.

Ngo knocked on the door before entering the room. He had a plate full of fried tofu with tomato sauce on the side. The snack was a perfect fit for their different dietary and taste palates. Davis and Alexandra were the first ones to get to the plate. Jazmine tried to grab a piece for herself, but each attempt met with it being stolen by either Davis or Alexandra.

"Madam Lee and Madam Gomez, your father is on the video call waiting for you two."

"Alright," Jazmine replied.

She got up from her chair and returned her book to the bag. She walked out of the room towards where the videophone was placed. Alexandra rushed to put her papers away so she would not be too far behind Jazmine.

Alexandra ran to catch up with her sister. Jazmine waited for her outside the door to the room where the call was. After Alexandra caught her breath, they walked into the room together. Their father was on the screen with a gentle smile. He had short blond and grey hair parted in the middle and pushed to the back. Logan wore a green striped suit with an orange bowtie. In the background, Logan's assistant was doing paperwork. She did not try to greet either Alexandra or Jazmine.

"Hello, my Jewels," Logan greeted.

"Hello, Father," Alexandra and Jazmine greeted in unison. "It is good to see you this afternoon."

"I expect that your studies and activities are going well."

"Yes, sir. Alexandra and I are at the top of our classes."

"We both also take pride in our work in the life maintenance and gymnastic clubs. I checked the grounds this afternoon, and it is safe to say everything is in order," Alexandra explained.

"How wonderful. I expect you to do your practice routines still, even though your season has ended, Jazmine. Just because others think they can slack off between seasons does not mean that you can."

"I wasn't planning on it, Father. Every day is a day for improvement."

"Perfect answer. I believe Ngo has already told you I will be away for several months. Until then, remember, society will advance in a positive way with hard work."

"Yes, sir," they agreed in unison. Ngo had never told them he would be gone for that long, but there was no point in voicing it. They assumed that their father pushed the date back and never told Ngo.

The video turned off soon after without a goodbye from either side. Alexandra and Jazmine let out a breath of relief. They could go back to their friends without any disruption. Jazmine took her time walking back to the game room while Alexandra sprinted back. She knew that Ji-yoon and Davis would finish eating the snacks if she did not. When Alexandra returned to the room, the snacks were already gone, as expected.

Chapter 2

The Journal

Around six-thirty, it was time for Ji-yoon and Davis to go home. Ngo took them home in the limo as it was their only option. Ji-yoon had to be dropped off first since the dorms were closer, and the dorms had a rule that students had to be inside by seven. Davis lived in town and had to be inside his house before his mother came home from work at seven-thirty. Ngo would return and start cooking dinner after he ensured their friends had made it home safely. This meant Alexandra and Jazmine were home alone for at least an hour.

Alexandra took this opportunity to catch up on paperwork for the life maintenance club and practice her Spanish. During this free time, Jazmine read a book. She had finished reading the book she had taken from her father's office. Usually, Jazmine would wait to read the journal the day after, but she couldn't wait. It wouldn't be a problem getting the next book.

Jazmine got the journals from her father's secret library in his office. Since he was rarely home, there was no chance he would notice one book disappearing and reappearing. The journals had different drawings that decorated the front of them to help show which one was made first. Jazmine had to ensure that Ngo did not catch her taking books out of the room or reading them. She did not want Ngo to tell her father about her entering one of his rooms. Out of the many rules she and Alexandra must follow, not going into their father's office was the top one. If Ngo caught them in one of their father's rooms, they would have less freedom than they already had.

Jazmine sneaked past Alexandra's room. Jazmine knew if her sister knew she was taking books from their father's room without permission that she would get mad. She didn't want to get a lecture from Alexandra if she could avoid it. It was more likely that Alexandra thought they were from a book series from the library.

The room she needed to go to was towards the back of the mansion. Steven locked the room from the outside. Jazmine believed that her father probably had the key on him to open the door and gave a copy to Ngo since nothing in the room seemed to ever gather dust based on the times Jazmine went in there. However, Jazmine found a way inside. Initially, it took her a few tries, but she unlocked the door with two bobby pins.

The room itself was nothing special. Jazmine looked at the hundreds of books that were placed on the bookcases. The journals that she was taking were not in either of them. Jazmine walked over to her father's desk and opened the bottom cabinet. There sat dozens of old journals. They all seemed to be written by the same person based on the handwriting, but she knew nothing more than that. She flipped through some of them to see the dates on the pages. Someone wrote the dates to tell the continuation of the journal that she needed.

"Bingo."

She replaced the old journal with the one that she needed. She shut the drawer before heading towards the door. Locking the door, Jazmine took her time to walk back to her room. She scanned through the book to see if there were any pictures in it. The woman who wrote the journals had drawings, and on rare occasions, someone would tape a photograph on the page. As she was flipping through it, a photo fell out of the journal, and someone else picked it up before she could.

"What's this?" Alexandra asked. She looked at the picture, confused. When Jazmine tried to take it back, Alexandra held the image above her head so that Jazmine could not reach it.

"Give it back!" Jazmine snapped. "It's none of your business."

"Everything you do is my business. Especially when there are no adults around. I have to look after you since you have less life experience than me."

"Since when? You're barely older than me!"

"But I'm still older," Alexandra reminded her. "So, what's this picture about? Is it the author or something?"

"As I said before," Jazmine started as she took back the picture, "it's none of your business."

Jazmine tried to walk away, but Alexandra stood in front of her. Jazmine tried to sidestep, but Alexandra would not let Jazmine get an inch away from her. Neither was about to go anywhere. Alexandra crossed her arms and smirked.

"What are you doing out of your room, anyway? We aren't supposed to be out of our room until dinner is ready."

"I went to the bathroom."

"We have those in our rooms. Try again."

"Well, why are you out of your room, then?"

"You have heavy footsteps. I could tell that you were out here."

"Or you were spying on me," Jazmine mumbled.

"What was that?"

"I'm just trying to read a book in peace. Is that so wrong, Alex? Because you do that every day."

Alexandra's eyes narrowed, and she snatched the picture back. "It is when you keep leaving your room when Ngo is gone, which has always been a rule for us. So, you either can tell me so I can lecture you, or I'll tell Ngo, and he'll do it."

"You know that you're the worst, right?"

Alexandra rolled her eyes and handed Jazmine back the picture. Jazmine put it back into the journal. Jazmine tried to go back to her room, but Alexandra stopped her again. She knew that Alexandra would not let the situation go so quickly.

Jazmine sighed. She pointed to Alexandra's room. She figured she would rather let Alexandra know her secret rather than Ngo because there was less chance of their father finding out. Worst case scenario, Jazmine would have to listen to her sister complaining about her taking the books for a couple of months.

Alexandra let Jazmine into her room first. Jazmine took a seat on Alexandra's bed while the older sibling sat at her desk. Alexandra closed the binder that was on her desk and turned toward Jazmine. She crossed her legs and gave her little sister her undivided attention. Jazmine let out a sigh before starting.

"You have to promise that you can't tell, alright?"

Alexandra was surprised. It was rare for Jazmine to ask her to keep a secret.

"Alright?"

"First off, it's not stealing if I am going to put it back after I'm done with it."

"Oh, my goodness, I'm telling Ngo," Alexandra warned. She tried to stand up, but Jazmine pushed her back into her seat.

"No! You just promised me."

"Fine, fine. But next time, don't start with that."

"Right," Jazmine answered. She gave Alexandra a closer look at the journal and the picture. "I found these journals in

Father's office. And all of them are handwritten. The adventures that this woman went on are amazing!"

"You should put it back. Father could be planning on publishing them for a friend."

"That's just it, Alex. So far, from what I read, he isn't mentioned at all, and these journals were written years ago, even before we were born."

"So?"

"So, why would he have something like this that dates so long ago and never publish it?" Jazmine questioned. "It doesn't make any sense. Especially what's written in them. It talks about magic and weird monsters."

"Maybe it's a memento? Like it's supposed to be a children's story or something similar," Alexandra answered. "But it doesn't matter. You broke into his room and took something that isn't yours."

Jazmine rolled her eyes. She laid back in the bed and mumbled something under her breath. Even though Alexandra claimed she would tell Ngo about borrowing the journals, Jazmine knew her sister better than that. It would be easy to get back on her good side. She rose from the bed with a grin.

"Don't worry, Alex, I promise that I won't take another one after this book. Just don't tell Ngo."

"You swear?"

"Yes! You know how I am. I just couldn't stop reading them; it makes me think about what I want to do with my life."

"It does? Well, that's great, but you do know magic isn't real, right?"

"Of course, magic isn't real."

Alexandra jumped out of her chair and pulled Jazmine into a bear hug. She could hear her sister squeak from the pain but ignored it. Alexandra went a step further and lifted Jazmine off the ground. Jazmine flailed her legs as a sign to be let go.

"Madams?"

"Oh, welcome back, Ngo," Alexandra greeted. She let go of Jazmine and let her sister flop onto her bed.

"What is going on here?" Ngo asked.

"Isn't it great, Ngo? Jazmine said that she would take the lead on the new student tours next semester."

"I did?" Jazmine questioned as she bolted up. Alexandra glared at her without losing the smile on her face. Jazmine knew she could say nothing to get out of it. She instead silently agreed with her sister.

"I understand. I will change the schedule for next semester," Ngo explained. "Dinner will be ready in half an hour."

Ngo bowed before taking his leave. After glaring at her sister for a few seconds, Jazmine returned to her room. She made sure not to leave behind the journal or the picture. Slamming the bedroom door would only cause Alexandra to come to scold her for it; instead, Jazmine yelled into her pillow after closing her door.

Jazmine decorated her room with pictures and merchandise of her favorite fictional characters. There was also random junk placed around the room. Since the room was so big, Jazmine put anything she could find into it to lessen the space.

Jazmine rolled around and faced her nightstand. She pulled open the top drawer and fumbled around until she felt a photo. While Jazmine usually placed the photos back into the journals, there was one that she could not put back. The picture that she held in her hand showed five teenagers sitting around a campfire. The person who caught Jazmine's attention was a dark skin Black woman that looked like she was having the most fun out of everyone. She was climbing over a Black man to get to a bag of chips that a tan woman with flowing black hair had. The man was trying to push her off him, and it looked like he was trying to hide his laughter with an annoyed face. The woman holding a bag was in the middle of rolling her eyes at them. On the other side of the campfire, a dark-skinned man with his hair tied into a bun was caring for a pale man who looked frightened at being outside in the woods at night. Jazmine did not know if the man was naturally pale or if he was that scared. Either way, it was good that the other man was there for him.

Jazmine could not understand why, but looking at the young woman's smile made her feel safe. She wished to ask her father more about this picture, especially the woman. The idea of getting into trouble with him was enough to stop her from asking. Jazmine didn't know if Ngo knew the people in the picture. He had been working for the family for as long as Jazmine could remember, so it would be reasonable to believe that he started around the time that her father was young.

July 14

Nights like these were the best. We are going on our next adventure in the morning, which I hope will end up better than the last place we visited. I wanted to go tonight, but they outvoted me. I hope they get their full hours of sleep because we aren't stopping once we are over there. This is bound to be the place where I find my talent.

"Talent?" Jazmine questioned.

Knock. Knock. Knock.

Jazmine jumped at the loud knocking. She quickly hid the journal in case the person came into her room. "Who is it?"

"Madam Lee," Ngo called from the other side of the door. "It is time for dinner."

"Coming!"

Jazmine placed the photo back inside her drawer. She wanted to ask Ngo if he knew about the picture, but there was no point in her getting two scoldings in one day. Asking Ngo would wait until winter break was over. She wanted to enjoy her break from school. Jazmine shot up from her bed when her door suddenly opened. Alexandra poked her head in.

"Time for dinner," Alexandra explained. "Ngo already told you that."

"It hasn't been ten seconds yet."

"I think Ngo would be extremely interested in where you find your books. Don't you think Jazmine?"

"See, this is the reason why you barely have any friends," Jazmine complained. "I already have to do that stupid tour next semester, and now you're doing this."

"Don't act like you're popular yourself. Now come on."

Jazmine mumbled something under her breath before following her. She purposely dragged her feet to make the walk to the dining room longer. At the end of each hallway, Alexandra had to wait for her. Alexandra knew if she said anything, that would just encourage Jazmine to go slower.

A three-minute walk to the dining room became ten. The dining room table could seat at least twenty people. Steven designed nothing in the mansion for the few people living there. Everything had to be ready in case a party would need to be held, even though he had never held a party in the mansion.

Alexandra and Jazmine took their usual spots at the table. It was near the entrance, but Jazmine sat on the opposite side of the table from Alexandra. Ngo placed each of their plates in front of them before disappearing into the kitchen. Jazmine picked at her rice while glaring at Alexandra, who happily ate her salmon. The quietness lasted for a few minutes before Jazmine decided to speak.

"I thought you liked doing your job?" she asked.

"I do, but I think it would be smart for you to make connections that will benefit the family. I can't do all that alone," Alexandra answered as she pushed the bitesize carrots off her plate.

"You just wanted to slack off," Jazmine mumbled.

Alexandra huffed at the accusation. "Plus, what's the worst that can happen?"

Jazmine knew that there would not be anything to change her sister's mind, so she accepted her role. The two changed the subject and talked about other aspects of school, such as classes and friends. Ngo checked on them multiple times throughout the dinner. Soon after that, the two had to go to their rooms for bed. Jazmine would usually have Alexandra review some of her homework, but since there was no work, she went to sleep early.

Chapter 3

Sleepless Night

Alexandra slipped out of her bed and walked towards her balcony. The layout of her room was relatively spacious but very cluttered. Instead of having multiple pieces of furniture placed around, Alexandra had her schoolwork and different foreign language books scattered everywhere. She walked over to one of her Korean books as she opened her balcony door. She welcomed the chilly breeze that the wind brought. The best part of living in the mountains to her was seeing the stars so clearly. Unlike in the city, the few lights in town did not take away the view.

The only sound that she could hear was the ticking of her cat wall clock. It was a few hours before Ngo would come wake her and Jazmine up for school. She couldn't understand what woke her up this early. She was usually a sound sleeper but had difficulty staying asleep tonight. It could not be because of exams because she felt the tests were easy and that she would pass them. As she thought of a reason for her restless sleep, Alexandra's thoughts went to the journal Jazmine had shown her earlier.

She knew better than to ask questions about it. Things always went wrong whenever someone asked questions that had nothing to do with them. This especially happened with her whenever Jazmine was involved. However, Alexandra knew she wouldn't have a good night's sleep unless she understood the journal. She slipped out of her room and down the hallway.

The hallway seemed longer at night because the only light source was the moonlight that came through the massive windows. Jazmine's room was not far away, situated on the other side of the hallway. There was no other room other than theirs on the floor. Since it was too late at night, Alexandra didn't believe that Ngo would be walking around the mansion. She peeked her head into her sister's room.

"Hey, Jazmine, are you awake?" Alexandra asked. She snuck into the room and gently closed the door behind her. Grabbing one of the many pillows that Jazmine had on her bed, Alexandra hit her sister in the face.

"Quit it!" Jazmine yelled as she ripped off her eye mask.

"Oh, great, you're up. That journal you were talking about earlier, I can't get it out of my head," Alexandra started as she plopped down next to her sister. "There something about them that doesn't make sense."

"Can't this wait until the morning?" Jazmine groaned.

"It is morning."

"It's three o'clock."

"It's not my fault that you go to sleep so late."

Jazmine grumbled something under her breath before sitting up. She fixed her bonnet and turned on her lamp. Alexandra was busy looking through one of her bedside drawers. When she couldn't find the journal in that one, Alexandra climbed over Jazmine to look at the other drawer.

Jazmine kicked her off. She went through her drawer to get the journal and tossed it to Alexandra. The elder sister scanned the book. She stopped when she got to a passage about a flower. There was an illustration of it on the next page. Alexandra held it up so that Jazmine could see it.

"Don't you recognize this flower?"

"I don't recognize many things this early in the morning," Jazmine shrugged.

Alexandra hit Jazmine's shoulder. She held the journal close to Jazmine's face so that she could see it better.

"Look closer then. We have seen this flower before."

The flower that Alexandra was talking about looked similar to a lotus flower. Yet, Jazmine did not know of any lotus flower with the color scheme that the book gave. It had different shades of green with little accents of brown. Thinking about it harder, Jazmine guessed Alexandra meant how the flower looked like their family crest. She then looked down at the description of the picture.

"The Flower of Nature," Jazmine read. "This flower helps bring plants to life in other dimensions. Every time a flower or something special comes up, it gets a description like this."

"So, you're telling me that something like this has come up before, and you thought nothing of it?"

"Is that a problem?"

"Don't you get it? I think that there's something more going on with this flower. Father isn't someone who would have books like this that talk about our worldly things," Alexandra explained. "And he doesn't even go around those types of people, yet he was close to someone who wrote those types of things."

"So what? You think this person is some sort of lost lover or something?" Jazmine asked. "And you complained that I read too many fantasy stories when you think he's capable of love."

"Jazmine!"

"When was the last time we saw him physically?"

Alexandra did not answer her sister and instead went back to the journal.

"Think about it. Legends and tall tales have some truth within them. These journals that you read are probably the same thing. On Saturday, we have to learn more about this. It is the only free day we have where Ngo isn't watching us, and we can even bring in Ji-yoon and Davis for this since school will be out for the break."

"I thought you didn't believe in magic."

"I don't, but if Father has something like this, it must be special!"

"Fine. Fine. Just let me sleep," Jazmine yawned before she turned away.

"I'll be studying this journal," Alexandra replied, "also, your bonnet is falling off."

Jazmine mumbled thanks before fixing her bonnet. Covering her eyes, she rolled over in her bed.

Alexandra turned off the light for her before slipping out of the room. She didn't know if or when Ngo would make his walk around the hallway. Sometimes it felt like the man didn't sleep. Alexandra rushed back into her room before he could catch her. If she couldn't fall back asleep, at least she could do some research from the journal.

The moon gave Alexandra enough light to use so that she would not have to turn on a lamp. The thought that she could find a plant her father had been looking for excited her. If she could discover it, then her father would surely be pleased. She tried to search on the internet to see where this specific lotus flower grew but found nothing. Searching the term "Flower of Nature" led to nothing as well.

Alexandra leaned back in her chair. She did not expect that she would get a hit right away, but for nothing to show up was disappointing. It had been over an hour since she started her research. Nothing in the books she had in her room had any information about this flower or any type of plant similar. She was going to need some extra help with figuring this out. Sighing, Alexandra texted Ji-yoon and Davis about the plan for Saturday. She did not expect a response since it was late at night. Yet, she knew who she could text that would reply to her instantly. Alexandra scanned through her contacts until she found the name Hua. She texted a simple hello, which resulted in a phone call.

"Lex! Hello! You never call me this late or, I guess, early," a cheerful voice answered.

"I told you not to call me that."

"Sorry. Do you need anything? Because I can help! Even if I have to look it up myself, I can help you."

"Hua didn't take botany this semester?"

"Yeah. Did you want to take it too? Why didn't you tell me? We could have done it together," Hua whined.

"I just wanted to know if you knew anything about lotus flowers, specifically my family crest?"

"I'm not thinking of anything off the top of my head, but when I see you in the committee room, I'll have figured out something by then."

"Thanks, I appreciate it."

"No pro-"

Alexandra hung up the phone before Hua could finish her sentence. She leaned back in her chair and groaned. She would rather not have any more help than was necessary. It was already annoying she could find nothing on her own, but it was also outside her area of expertise. The classes she usually took related to either business or humanities. Alexandra did not expect knowing about plants would be necessary for her life.

Alexandra took one last look at the picture of the teenagers around a campfire that she found in the journal. She tried to examine each of them carefully. Her father had no friends she knew of, so these people had to be frequent work acquaintances. There were no other options. Since she had read none of the journals before, she had to figure out how each person's relationship with each other.

From right to left, Alexandra figured that the woman reaching for the bag and the man she was on top of were siblings. They had similar features and attitudes that resembled her relationship with Jazmine.

"He probably actually cares for her," she thought.

The other woman in the photo looked used to the oddness around her. She wasn't even paying attention to the others as she tried to give away a bag of chips. The pale man looked like he needed help. It seemed like he was often going to die from fright since there was only one person trying to help him. When Alexandra inspected the man helping him, she realized she recognized him or at least someone that looked similar.

"No way."

A knock on the door made Alexandra jump out of her seat. There was no way that Jazmine would be up at this time or at least want to enter her room. Unfortunately, that left only one person. She tried to stay quiet, hoping he would think she was still asleep.

"Madam, is everything alright?" Ngo questioned. "You aren't supposed to be up at this time."

"Y-yes!" she stuttered. "Just had a nightmare, that's all."

"Would you like a glass of water?"

"No, thank you. I think I'm just going to go back to bed."

"If that is what you wish. I will come back to check on you."

"Thank you, Ngo."

She quickly packed the journal and the picture in her backpack before jumping into bed. She heard Ngo's footsteps when she was back in her bed. He was walking away, and he would check on Jazmine next. Alexandra knew she could do nothing else for the rest of the night. The worst part about Ngo interrupting her was that her heart was beating too fast, so she would not get back to sleep for some time.

The thoughts of the man from the picture filled her mind. He had gentle hazel eyes that she was sure she had seen before. The main thing that threw off her theory was that she had met this man before. He had a scare that ran down the side of his face. This was a feature that needed to be remembered.

"He has to be someone's relative then because there's no way that it could actually be him," she thought.

The more she thought about the man, the more frustrated she became. There would be no way that her father would be around someone with something like that on his face. She did not know how the man got such a large scar on his face, but since her father valued perfection, it was something that he would not overlook.

"Jazmine would be no help with this since she couldn't even figure out that our family crest is based on this strange lotus," Alexandra thought. She turned to her side and tried to salvage some rest before getting ready for school in the morning. A mystery would not ruin her school record.

***

Tossing and turning, Jazmine could not fall back asleep. Alexandra came into her room over an hour ago to talk about the journal she had taken from her father's office. She did not fully listen to Alexandra, but she was sure that it was something important.

Jazmine could hear Ngo's footsteps coming close to her room. He usually would be at her door a few minutes earlier. She wondered what could have made him run behind. Ngo was always the one to be on time for things. Jazmine breathed a little louder to mimic how she sounded when she was asleep. She could tell that Ngo was listing through the door before he turned to leave.

"Predictable," she thought.

Jazmine sat up and scanned her room, waiting for her eyes to adjust to the darkness. Jazmine's bed sat in the middle of

54

the room, allowing her to see everything simultaneously. Unlike Alexandra, Jazmine kept her room neat for the most part. She had her own mini library on the right side of her room and the books that did not fit onto the shelves were stacked neatly near by. The study desk she used sat near her balcony so she could look out the window while doing her work.

On the left side of her room, Jazmine had set up a bulletin board mounted on the wall. She filled it with pictures of her friends and family. There were plenty of pictures scattered around the board of her and Alexandra as children playing with Ngo. Then there were pictures of her in her dancing uniform after a performance. Davis had dozens of photos with her, as well as Ji-yoon. Another friend of hers, Michael, was photo-bombing different selfies that Hua was trying to take.

Jazmine crawled out of her bed. She walked to her balcony and pushed one side of the curtain away, but not too far, as she did not want any moonlight to peek through her door into the hallway. Sliding through the door, the balcony had only a purple bench as decoration. Jazmine sat on the bench and looked up at the sky. It was not uncommon for her to be up this late at night, but she never took the time to look outside.

Living in the mountains, Jazmine could see the stars clear as day. The crescent moon shined brightly against the purplish-black sky. She could not see the city from the angle of her balcony but had the perfect forest view. It was miles away from the mansion. No one has entered it since it has been chained off for years.

The forest was so lush that it was hard to see anything. Even though it was night, Jazmine thought she could see some type of animal coming from it, be it an owl or some type of night bird. Yet, there was nothing. Nothing in the forest felt alive, but that could not be right. There had to be something in there waiting to explore outside the fence. They were probably sad to see the same thing every day, which was something Jazmine could relate to. It was already rare for her to see any type of animal that came anywhere other than the science room because of her being confined in either school or home. The idea of something going through the same thing made Jazmine emotional.

"This must be what zoo animals feel like," she thought.

She tried to take her mind off how depressing life was by thinking about the people in the photo and all the journals.

Alexandra seemed sure of something regarding them, which was interesting since she had only seen one picture and book. It would be a lie to say that Jazmine could not see the connections to everything but only decided to say something to her sister now. The picture of the group of teens made her want to show someone as it was the first clear photo of them all together.

The pictures in past journals showed them individually, if the person could get them to take one. Jazmine remembered one photo of a guy blocking the camera so that it could not get a shot of him. In another, they had a type of face paint on, which made it harder for her to see who it was.

The worst part was that there weren't names of to the people in the pictures. Jazmine did not know why the writer would do that, but there were times when it felt that their names were purposely erased from the journals. Knowing that she would get nowhere tonight thinking about the mysteries of the journals, she went back into her room. She did not want to get in trouble with her teacher for falling asleep in class right before winter break.

Chapter 4

Commuting

Around six-thirty, Davis skimmed through the radio channels to find a station to play in his mother's car. He expected little since it was early morning, and none of the good radio hosts were on. He was waiting for his mom to get in to drive him to school. The hospital had called her in early, which meant she had to take him to school before started. Davis was used to this, since having a parent in the medical field usually called at random shift times. When he decided that no good music was playing on the radio, Davis looked through his phone.

"Ready to go?" his mother asked as she hopped into the car. She grabbed her badge, which stated her name, Tanisha Brown, hanging from the rearview mirror.

"Yes, ma'am."

Tanisha had similar features to her son, such as a small birthmark on their neck. She had her braids tied into a bun and had a half-eaten bagel in her mouth. Davis expected her to put on her makeup while driving since they were in a rush. She already had an extra pair of work shoes in the back seat in case of emergencies like this.

"I forgot my lunch!" Tanisha exclaimed.

"I put it in the backseat next to your shoes," Davis pointed out.

"Alrighty then. I might stay over a little late tonight, but there still should be leftovers for you to eat."

"Alright. Hey Mom, is it cool if I hang out with friends on Saturday?" Davis asked. He had just found a text message from Alexandra that was sent around four in the morning. He did not know which was weirder, her texting at such a late hour or her texting him at all. Alexandra was not much of a texter.

"If your room is clean, then fine."

"Thanks."

The two of them continued to talk about other things, such as what was going on at the hospital and how Davis's friends were doing. It took them about fifteen minutes to make it to the front of the school, even though it was about an hour's drive from their house. He did not know how his mom and Ngo being the two most responsible adults he knew were so quick to break speeding laws. Davis kissed his mother on the cheek before leaving the car.

"Davis! You almost forgot your ball!" she yelled.

Davis caught the soccer ball that his mom threw out the window. She gave him one last wave before speeding off. Davis thought he should go to the soccer field since he had nowhere else to go. It was good that he still had an extra uniform in his locker that he could change into.

Davis took his time to walk to the soccer field. There should be no one there until seven-thirty. This gave him time to practice his shooting. He realized he should text Alexandra back first. A football slamming into him snapped him out of his thought process. It took a moment for his vision to fix itself.

"Come on, dude, you know you're supposed to catch it."

Davis looked up to see the school's football star, Michael Huang. Michael was wearing his school uniform, which Davis felt was too tight for him. Davis could see his muscles perfectly outlined by his shirt. Michael's tan skin shined in the early morning glow. Davis had to admit that Michael's hazel eyes looked kind and beautiful. It was almost hard for Davis to look away. Michael had his bag hanging from his shoulder and his necklace with his birthstone, a pearl, around his neck. Michael had his hair in his usual spike-up hairstyle that Davis was sure took him too long to make perfect.

It was still too early for class to begin, so Davis assumed he was there for morning detention. Michael had his usual grin plastered on his face. Davis could tell that his plans for this morning were already out the window, not that he minded much.

"Let me help you up," Michael offered.

"No thanks, I can do it myself."

"Aw, come on."

Michael took it upon himself to pick Davis up. Davis was glad that it was too early for students to be here because he wouldn't be able to handle the embarrassment of being picked up so easily by another man. The worst part was Michael refused to put him down.

Davis huffed. "Put me down, Michael."

"But my neck always hurts from down at you when we talk."

"Then don't talk to me."

"I don't know who that would hurt more. Me or you?"

Davis hid a smile at the comment. Michael laughed before putting Davis down. Davis continued his walk to the soccer field but realized Michael was following him. He was humming a new song that he heard. Davis sighed because he knew that detention left his mind.

"Don't you have somewhere to be?"

"Yeah, Mrs. Kane gave me dentition yesterday for eating in class. Lame, right?"

"Couldn't wait until lunch?"

"Oh, I had her after lunch, but I was still hungry. You get it by being an athlete yourself, right? Oh yeah, you've got to invite me to your games when the spring comes. I heard that your first years are surprisingly good."

"We have to be if we want to play. Plus, you have practice during our game."

"I can skip a practice or two. But yeah, the school is pretty strict about who plays. Even second-year students like me have a tough time being able to play games. Well, not me, since I'm amazing."

Davis rolled his eyes. He wouldn't be Michael if he didn't boast about himself. He hoped that his mother didn't have to go in early tomorrow because it looked like Michael was going to be in detention again since he wasn't about to go there today. Michael tended to stop whatever he was doing to be with Davis.

Noticing the soccer ball, Michael took Davis's ball out of his hand. He claimed he knew how to dribble it with his feet. He didn't. Michael tried his best to move the ball how he wanted. Davis watched him fail a few more times before stepping in and helping. Davis first showed him how it was supposed to look. When Michael could not copy it, Davis helped move Michael's legs into the correct position. Michael hummed in enjoyment at the physical contact.

"You pretend to be bad at things too much," Davis complained.

"Yet, you still help me."

Davis headed to the classrooms first. Michael was so busy trying to get Davis's attention that he didn't notice that he was headed toward where his detention was happening. He realized they'd entered building halfway through the first hallway.

"When did we get in here?"

"You've got to start paying attention."

"Well, I pay attention to you."

"I'll accept that."

Michael bent down and nuzzled his head into Davis's neck. Davis softly laughed and rubbed Michael's head. The taller teen pouted at the action. It took Michael a long time to get his hair how he wanted. He quickly fixed it when he heard footsteps coming towards them. An older woman with a clipboard walked out of a classroom. She wore a skirt suit and had her hair tied into a neat bun. Even with the wrinkles around her eyes, it was easy to tell that the woman had a young heart. She turned towards them and smiled. She happily marked something off on the clipboard before moving away from the door.

"It's great that you can finally make it, Mr. Huang."

"Oh, hello, ma'am," Michael greeted. "See you later, Davis."

Michael walked into the classroom to serve his morning dentition. Davis gave him a quick bye. He was about to leave when the teacher called his name.

"I would like to thank you for bringing Mr. Huang to me."

"It was my pleasure."

"It's good that he has such a responsible boyfriend like yourself."

"W-what?" Davis choked. He flailed his arms to say no since the words could not come out of his mouth. "We're just friends."

"It's alright. I might be old, but I am up to date with the world these days. Do you know that old saying that you can't teach an old dog new tricks? Well, I think that's some malarkey." The woman let out a hearty laugh. She patted Davis on the back relentlessly.

"Whatever you say, ma'am."

Davis quickly got away from the teacher. Every time he had to talk to her, she would say saying something like that if he was around Michael. He checked his phone and saw he still had time to himself before school started. Since he had practice for his first period, Davis changed into his uniform before leaving the building. Davis couldn't get any early morning practice in because Michael kept sending him pictures of himself. He chuckled and sent photos of himself back to him. Between

receiving texts, Davis called Ji-yoon to ensure she was awake.

Chapter 5

School Mates

In the student dorms, Ji-yoon was startled awake by the sound of her phone ringing. She reached for the phone and saw that Hua was calling to wake her up. She answered the phone with some jumbled-up words before hanging up. It took her a moment. Ji-yoon dragged herself out of bed. In a daze, she stared into the darkness before opening her curtains. Ji-yoon felt like the sunlight had almost blinded her by its sheer power.

She walked over to the front of her room to turn on her light to adjust better to the early morning. It was their last day for the semester, and Ji-yoon wanted nothing more than to slip back into her bed. Unwillingly, she changed into her school uniform. Ji-yoon glanced at her phone and noticed Alexandra had sent her something on the group chat.

"I was hoping to sleep in tomorrow," she mumbled.

Ji-yoon knew her friend well. Even though she did not give a time to come over, Ji-yoon knew that if Alexandra did not provide a detailed explanation, it was secretive and important to her. It would be best to come as early as possible, but Ji-yoon could always ask more about it when she saw Alexandra in the committee room.

When she got dressed, Ji-yoon's notification system on her computer went off. She was getting a video message invite. Only one person would call her this early in the morning. Ji-yoon hopped onto her computer and accepted the call. A young girl in a different school uniform appeared on the screen. She looked remarkably similar to Ji-yoon aside from having a narrower nose and being a shade lighter. The girl seemed to be outside somewhere and was using her phone to talk to Ji-yoon.

"Sister! How are you doing?"

"I'm fine. It seems your English classes are doing well, Yujin," Ji-yoon commented.

Instead of speaking in English, Ji-yoon was speaking in her native tongue, Korean. While she knew it was good for her sister to practice her English, Ji-yoon instead spoke in Korean as she could not in school. No one stopped her from speaking it, but the problem was that only a few people spoke it fluently. The other students that came from Korea did not talk to her because she was half-Korean. Even though she was born in Korea and had a Korean father, she looked too much like her African American mother to be seen as Korean by them. The Korean Americans who could speak the language could not relate to parts of Ji-yoon's life.

Alexandra tried to speak in Korean whenever she noticed that Ji-yoon felt out of place. Alexandra was far from being fluent since she had only been learning for a semester and was also currently learning Spanish. Sometimes she would accidentally speak Spanish for a word she did not know in Korean. Ji-yoon was okay with the mismatch of language. Alexandra's trying was good enough for her. Plus, this was how she learned a few phrases in Spanish.

Yujin raised one of her arms in excitement. "You would not believe what happened. Min-jun got accepted into Seoul National University."

"Oh. That's nice."

"Yeah! Dad is going to get him that new virtual reality system that just came out, and Mom has been bragging to anyone that will listen."

Ji-yoon had to force herself to not roll her eyes. While Ji-yoon loved her older brother, she could not stand hearing about him. Every time someone mentioned him, it had to be about something spectacular he did. He can do nothing wrong, especially to their parents. He was why she left the country for school and was not going back during the break.

Ji-yoon understood that getting into Seoul National University was a dream that anyone in Korea would kill for, but she was doing fantastic academically as well. She had taught herself English to have an edge in getting into Silver Valley. Neither of her parents helped her as they did with her brother. The only thing that she got for being accepted was a halfhearted thank you.

"How has everything been for you?" Ji-yoon asked. She wanted to get far away from the subject of Min-jun.

"Well, I've been doing well in my classes, but I'm nowhere near the level you and big brother are."

"You don't have to compare yourself to us. There are things you can do that we can't, like singing. Min-jun is tone-death, and I can't carry a pitch even if you paid me."

Yujin giggled at Ji-yoon's statement. "I wish you could come home to spend Christmas with us."

"Yeah, I do too, but you know, got to get ahead on my schoolwork."

"Don't forget to take regular breaks. Oh! I can send you some snacks from over here as a present. I even tried to make you some food, grandma's recipe."

"Thanks. You know, for a school that supports diversity, it does not have good Korean food."

"That's terrible."

"You're telling me."

The two of them continued to talk for a while until Ji-yoon heard a knock on the door. This showed that it was time for her to head to school. She gave her sister a quick goodbye before ending the call.

Ji-yoon grabbed her bag and opened the door to see her classmate Hua Huang waiting for her. She was a relatively short girl compared to the others at school. It could be because she was

71

one of the youngest, as she could enroll in the school a year early because of her intelligence. Hua was carrying a large book about plants, and a blueberry muffin was on top of it.

"Morning, Ji-yoon." Hua greeted her.

Hua was a pale girl who wore the uniform color of the maintenance club. She wore a cardigan like Ji-yoon, but it seemed like Hua's cardigan was too big for her, with glasses just as big. Ji-yoon wondered why Hua was wearing her glasses because she usually put in her green color contacts when they went to school. Hua had her long hair in a half-up, half-down pigtail style.

Pushing her glasses up, Hua gave Ji-yoon a smile. "Ready for the last day of this semester?"

"Words can't describe how ready."

"Then let's go."

Ji-yoon took the muffin she knew was for her, and the two of them went outside. Other students passed them, and Ji-yoon could tell that some of them planned to skip the last day. This would cause them to have a week's worth of dentition when the spring semester started. The lack of students going to school did not bother Ji-yoon because it meant fewer people would be on the bus. When the two of them got on the bus, Hua told Ji-yoon why she had such a large book about plants on their last day of the semester.

"That explains her text, then."

"Huh? She asked you about it too?" Hua said.

"Well, she only texted me about coming over to her house tomorrow to help her with something."

"She didn't ask me to come over," Hua whined. Ji-yoon chuckled at Hua's attitude about being forgotten. She placed her hand on Hua's head.

"Just show up then."

"I can't just show up at someone's house unannounced."

"It's fine. Plus, you will be with me, and if things go south, just say that Jazzy invited you. She's fine with going against Lex."

"I guess."

"If you're really worried, then ask Lex herself when you see her."

Hua made a small noise, signaling that she would. She raised her feet up and laid against Ji-yoon. The older teen allowed her since it would take them only a short time to make it to the school gates. The ride to school was less eventful than usual because of the lack of students. Ji-yoon feared she would have to wait until the end of the school day for her to find out what Alexandra wanted to know about a plant and that she would need help from multiple people to figure it out.

Unfortunately for Ji-yoon, she did have to wait until the end of the day. Alexandra refused to talk about anything, yet she wanted to. Ji-yoon watched her friend as she fidgeted in her seat during their math class. During their last committee meeting, Alexandra said nothing and made her take over. Hua tried to show her the book, but she brushed her off and told her she could show it later. When asked, Jazmine did not know what was going through Alexandra's mind, either. She could only give what little she knew to Ji-yoon during their science class.

They, along with Davis, were sitting around a table that had a Bunsen burner on it. Since they had no work to do, the three of them were roasting marshmallows over the burner. The only other people in the classroom were the teacher and five more students. Figuring that Alexandra had a big secret, they kept their voices low so no one else could hear them.

"Yeah, she was acting weird last night, but it was more exciting, weird," she explained. "Since this morning, it has just been straight-up weird."

"All of that over a book you stole?" Davis questioned.

"Borrowed," Jazmine quickly corrected.

"There must be something else to it. Jazzy, besides the flower, was there anything else that would be recognizable?" Ji-yoon quizzed. "If you overlooked something small as a flower, then there could be something else."

Jazmine shrugged. "I dunno. There was a picture that had some people that felt familiar to me, but that's about it."

"Knowing her, she probably won't show us the picture till tomorrow," Davis commented.

"How are you not questioning her behavior about all of this? Especially you, Jazzy," Ji-yoon grilled.

"Not everyone is nosey like you," Jazmine responded. "I'm fine with waiting until someone gives the gossip to me, so I don't have to hunt for it."

Ji-yoon clicked her tongue at the statement. The three of them diverted the conversation into a mixture of random nonsense. During Ji-yoon's last class, she received a text message from Alexandra. She wanted to meet Ji-yoon in the committee room. It turned out the others received the exact text as well. Yet, she did not know why Michael was there. He was sitting in a chair off to the side.

"I didn't realize that she had your number," Ji-yoon admitted.

"She doesn't. I planned on going out for dinner with my sister, but she said she had to stop by here first."

Hua nodded. She was showing the plant book to Alexandra. It seemed as if whatever she wanted to know wasn't in the book after all. Alexandra slammed the book closed and shoved it back at Hua. Michael gave her an annoyed look that she ignored.

"There is nothing about that specific flower," Alexandra finally spoke.

"Your family's lotus flower, right?" Davis questioned.

"You told him?"

"Alex, you can't expect to give people a cryptic message and for them to not have answers," Jazmine explained.

Alexandra huffed. Yet again, Jazmine did something without her permission or knowledge. Davis nervously rubbed the back of his head. He could tell that Alexandra was getting mad. Fidgeting his hands, Davis tried to think of something to say, but before he could, Alexandra spoke.

"How much does he know?" she asked.

"Well, Davis and I know as much as Jazzy knows," Jiyoon piped in.

"Fine then," Alexandra groaned. "You two need to come to the mansion as early as possible tomorrow."

"You're really gonna leave us suspense like that, aren't you?" Jazmine questioned.

"Davis, when is the quickest that you can get to the mansion?" Alexandra asked, completely ignoring her sister.

"I don't know. It depends on when my mom gets off work. If she's just getting off, she shouldn't be driving while tired," Davis explained. "If she's already asleep, I don't want to wake her."

"I have an idea that could get Davis to you guys early. He can just ask his mom to let him stay over at my dorm tonight," Michael suggested. "The dorms will be mostly empty due to people going home for the break."

"Brilliant! Davis, call her right now!" Alexandra demanded.

Davis's mouth moved as if trying to speak, but no words came out. Michael's plan sounded great, and Davis knew he was doing it out of kindness and nothing else. The only thing Davis would have to do if his mother said yes would be pick up his clothes and head over to Michael's room. Davis turned to Jazmine to see if she understood his hesitance. She gave him a sly smile.

"Give me a minute," Davis said as he stepped outside so that he could try to call his mother.

"Now, while he's on the phone," Michael began, "Hua and I will come over tomorrow as well."

"Excuse me?" Alexandra questioned. "And why do you think that you're coming over?"

"Well, you're using me as a way for Davis to lie to his mother he loves so very much," Michael explained. "Plus, you technically put my little sister into this by asking for her help. I feel like we should find out what's going on, too."

"Michael, do you even care?"

"No, not really. So, are we invited?"

"No."

"Jazz."

"Sure, I don't care if you come."

Alexandra glared at her sister, who paid no mind. Jazmine always tried to undermine her decisions. Alexandra crossed her arms, knowing that Michael and Hua would now show up. She wanted as few people as possible to know about what was going on. Not only would it lower the prestige it would give her for her findings since she already had to share it with Jazmine, Ji-yoon, and Davis, but she was also far from Michael's friend.

Hua tugged at her skirt as she studied Alexandra's face. She did not want to make her mad. Alexandra clicked her tongue before taking a seat far from Michael. She did not hide her annoyance. Michael and Jazmine laughed at Alexandra's attitude. Hua did not want Alexandra to think that she and her brother were pushing her to do something she did not wish to do it. Before Hua could say anything to Alexandra, Davis came back into the room and gave a thumbs-up.

"See," Michael called out. "My plan worked out perfectly."

"Now," Ji-yoon started, "can we find out what's going on?"

"I have to tell you tomorrow."

"Alex."

"I do. If I tell you now, Jazmine is going to act weird for the rest of the day, and I can't have that with Ngo around. Everyone be at the mansion at nine."

"Pretty sure that you're mistaking me for you,"

"In the morning?" Ji-yoon questioned.

Alexandra glared at her before picking up her bag. She did not answer the questions her friends were asking her. Jazmine sighed and followed her. When Alexandra got in a mood like this, Jazmine found it better to let her work it out herself. She knew her sister was the type who snapped at anyone, even those who were trying to help.

The two of them fixed their composure when they met Ngo at the front of the building. The last thing that either of them wanted was to make him suspicious. He could either stop whatever Alexandra was planning on doing or, worse, tell their father about their strange actions.

Davis caught up with them before they drove off. He needed a ride home so that he could pack his things. Ngo was kind enough to wait at Davis's house so that he could drive him back to the school.

"It is rare for him to want to spend the night somewhere else," Ngo commented.

"Yeah, I believe he is going to practice with some friends later on," Alexandra lied.

"He's very serious about soccer," Jazmine added.

Ngo nodded and dropped that subject as Davis had just come out of his house. Jazmine was thankful that she came to Davis's house and was not dropped off at home earlier because she wouldn't have been able to see the city. Neither she nor Alexandra came down the mountain often. They were not allowed to because it would go against their father's plan of keeping them hidden from the world.

Davis took the time to point out different shops for her and Alexandra. He made sure to avoid talking about their plan in front of Ngo. Davis knew he would find nothing else out until tomorrow, even if Ngo was not there.

Ngo drove back to the school to drop off Davis. Waiting for him, Michael was relaxing against a wall. He did not react to the car until it entirely stopped. As he was not well acquainted with Ngo, he gave him an awkward wave as a greeting. Michael grabbed some bags that Davis was carrying.

"Sorry I took so long," Davis apologized.

"It's not a problem. The girls already took the bus back to the dorms, though."

"Mr. Brown, would you like for me to take you and your friend to the living dorms?" Ngo asked.

"Nah, we'll be fine," Davis replied. He turned towards Michael. "We're super close. I'm probably his favorite after Jazzy and Alex."

Seeing Ngo rolling his eyes, Michael did not want to correct him. "But at least I'm still your favorite," he teased.

Davis could hear Jazmine giggling from the car. Michael's grin grew more prominent at Jazmine's encouragement. Davis did not know how to reply to that, especially in front of people. Ngo returned to the car.

"See you all tomorrow!" Davis yelled from the car.

Michael waved. "Well, time to head off. Don't worry; my room is already clean."

Davis nodded as he felt his mouth go dry. As they walked up the mountain, Michael talked about random topics. Davis did not know if he was doing this to fill the silence or if Michael did not realize he was jumping around topics. Davis would skip around in the conversation if it was himself because he could not keep his thoughts straight.

"Have you ever been to the dorms before?" Michael asked.

"Some of my teammates have shown me pictures of their rooms."

"Well, my room is going to be ten times better than theirs," Michael cooed.

It took him some time, but Davis opened up to Michael. When Michael toned down his flirting, Davis found it easier to continue the conversation with him. After fifteen minutes of walking, they made it to the student dorms. Davis was amazed at the size of the building.

The parking lot lay to the left of the building, and Davis could see a few buses and cars there. The building was pale yellowish brown but had plenty of flowers and other plant life

around the area. There were a few students waiting outside the

building with their bags. Davis guessed they were leaving for the

break. He followed behind Michael as they navigated the

hallways.

The students still in the building greeted them as if they

knew them. It did not take them long to get to Michael's dorm.

The school allowed the students related to each other to live

together in their own apartment-style dorm. When they reached

the door, Davis could hear voices on the other side. He saw the

smile drop from Michael's face.

Michael opened the door against his best wishes. Ji-yoon

was sitting on the couch with a silent television playing in the

background. She saw them and waved. Hua was on the other side

of the room on a laptop. She was talking to two people. Davis

could clearly hear the conversation that Hua was having the

farther he walked into the room, but before he could enter fully,

he had to take off his shoes as per Michael's wishes.

"Who was that?" a feminine voice asked.

Hua looked up at her brother. Michael pointed at himself

before heading off to the kitchen. Hua looked back at the

computer. Davis could tell how uncomfortable Hua felt. She tugged on her skirt before answering.

"It was Chen."

Davis was surprised that she used Michael's real name. He knew Michael had no problem using his birth name, but rarely used it since he came to the school. It was to the point where people did not know that he had another name. At the school, the Asian students usually used their birth name as encouraged instead of their Americanized name because the faculty claimed that using their birth name helped with the connection with others.

"You need to go home," a muscular voice commanded.

"Dad, I'll be fine. Talk to you and Mom later," Hua replied.

Davis heard the man try to argue until Hua ended the call. Michael came back into the room soon after. He handed Davis a water bottle before taking a seat next to Ji-yoon. Davis wanted to ask what the call was about but decided it would be better not to.

"I think it would be better if we get something from the cafeteria," Hua pointed out. "I don't feel like walking down the mountain to get something to eat."

"Fine by me. We can bring what we get back here."

"I'm coming too," Ji-yoon said. "I have my school card on me. What about you, Davis?"

"Yeah."

Michael decided he wanted to change out of his uniform before leaving, and Hua had to grab her school card from her room. The second that they left the room, Davis sat next to Ji-yoon. She already knew what he was about to ask her.

"Michael doesn't get along with his parents."

"Really? But Michael gets along with everybody."

"That's the weird part."

"Do you know why?"

"Nope, and Hua won't tell me either."

"I'm surprised that you haven't tried to grill her about it."

"Hey, I enjoy having the scoop as much as the next person, but I draw the line at family drama."

Hua came back into the room first and Michael soon after. Davis had never been to the cafeteria in the student dorm before. There were a few students sitting at random tables while others were taking their food to go. Getting the food was easier than Davis thought it would be. It was just like how he had to order food during school hours. There were more alternative food choices compared to the school lunch, however.

Davis noticed it did not take Michael long to return to his usual bubbly self. He was grateful for that. While Michael could talk too much, Davis preferred that than him being in a bad mood.

"There is no way that you're going to be satisfied with just a salad," Michael commented on Hua's dinner selection.

"Just because I don't eat an insane amount of meat like you doesn't mean that I'm not full," she rebutted.

As Ji-yoon said, Michael had several types of meat on his to-go plate. He had some vegetables and fruit in there as well. Davis's plate was like Michael's, but he had a smaller amount of meat on his plate. Ji-yoon's plate had the perfect proportions of food but had many desserts in a separate bag.

Davis enjoyed his time at the dorms. He could usually only spend time at Jazmine and Alexandra's place because his mother worked at random times. Ji-yoon left around eight. She claimed she had go to sleep early if she wanted to have enough energy for tomorrow. Hua went to bed around ten.

"You can take my bed if you want," Michael said.

"I'm fine on the couch."

"Dude, you're my guest. My room is clean, so don't worry about that."

Davis figured Michael would not drop the idea. Michael's room was not decorated as Davis thought it would be. He did not know if it was because the school owned the room, but most of the things Michael had hanging on the wall stayed there because of tape. There was little color in the room. Davis left the door open just in case Michael needed something. He stared at the ceiling as he lay in Michael's bed.

The only thing that Davis could hear was the living room's television playing softly in the background. He had never slept over in someone else's place before. The idea of sleeping in an unfamiliar place made him uncomfortable. Yet, Davis drifted off to sleep a few minutes after bed.

Chapter 6

Additional Issues

Jazmine had watched her sister make a fool out of herself for the past couple of hours. Alexandra had acted strange around Ngo the moment that she had seen him yesterday. She made it evident that she was hiding something as she could barely talk to him throughout dinner. Breakfast wasn't any better. However, Alexandra managed to tell him they were going out with their friends today but left out where they were going.

While in Alexandra's room, Jazmine watched as she continued to stuff things into her backpack. The items ranged from the journal to medical supplies. Alexandra wanted Jazmine to pack her own bag with similar things. Jazmine, however, packed her bag full of food. She knew her sister would forget something as important as that.

Jazmine was told what type of outfit she should wear for their outing. Jazmine had on a purple with grey stars short-sleeved shirt and black jeans. She was told to wear a pair of comfortable shoes, so she went with a pair of purple tennis shoes that she had not been able to wear yet.

Alexandra wore an oversized red T-shirt tied to the side and shorts that came down to her knees. Jazmine noticed that the type of boots that Alexandra was wearing were perfect for walking long distances and gave more inches to her towering height.

"Tell me, why are we packing these bags again? Aren't we staying here so that you can talk to us?" Jazmine asked.

"I can't talk about my discovery here. Ngo can't know that you were sneaking into Father's room."

"Then hurry. Davis said that they'll be here in five minutes."

"Right, that's everything. Come on, Ji-yoon texted me earlier that they should be here any minute."

"And you complain about me not listening?"

Alexandra glared at her before walking out of the room. Jazmine rolled her eyes before following her sister to the main entrance. Ngo was already in the room when they came in. He was busy cleaning the windows so that he could see when the guests were coming. As Alexandra and Jazmine expected, their friends were walking to the front door.

"I hope you two have a splendid time out," Ngo said.

"We will," they replied.

Jazmine opened the door and saw that Davis was seconds away from knocking on it. The others were behind him. Ji-yoon and Hua were the only ones who had bags on them, which were their purses. Jazmine realized that no one told them they should have brought something. In her defense, Jazmine did not know where Alexandra would take them.

Alexandra grabbed her sister's hand and pulled her out of the door. Jazmine barely had the chance to catch the bag Ngo tossed at her. Davis waved hello to Ngo before chasing after his friends. Ji-yoon and Hua did the same thing, though Hua was shyer with her greeting.

Davis wore a light blue long-sleeve shirt and jeans. Since he was not in school, Davis was allowed to wear his blue and black tennis shoes. Jazmine was sure that his mother made him wear a long sleeve shirt even though the weather was nice enough to not have one. He always told her how his mother did not take any chances regarding his health.

Jazmine had never seen Michael or Hua outside of school before. Surprisingly, the Huang siblings were more fashionable than Jazmine thought they would be. Michael seemed to be dressed in athletic wear. He had a grey hoodie with his number twenty-four on it and shorts that came to his knees. Michael and Davis wore sneakers, which looked comfier than the heels that Hua and Ji-yoon had on.

Hua had a cute aesthetic going on with her outfit. She did not have on her glasses, but Jazmine knew Hua had them in her purse. Compared to her brother, Hua had more of a cute aesthetic for her clothing. She wore an oversized pink and white T-shirt with a short skirt. Even with her heels on, she was still the shortest in the group. Jazmine noticed that she decided to use her teddy bear purse today.

Ji-yoon's style was consistent with what Jazmine had seen her wear before. She wore mute colors, and her outfit was well taken care of. Jazmine knew that Ji-yoon rarely bought clothes since she had been in the country. It could be because she liked the style choices of Korea better. She wore a dull yellow tube top with blue khaki pants. With her wedge heels, Jazmine could guess they were around the same height now.

Besides Michael's mom not making him bring one, the lack of jackets did not surprise Jazmine. Even though they lived in the mountains, and it was winter, it never got too cold for anyone to want to wear a jacket or coat. She never understood why. Other cities this high up would have been snowing by now.

"Wait a minute, we just got here," Michael whined.

"Shut up," Alexandra whispered, placing her hand over Michael's mouth. "We're going out like we said we would."

Ngo looked at them with no emotion. Alexandra was sure that he had heard Michael. If he said nothing about it, then she would not question it. Michael tried to voice his displeasure, but Alexandra dragged him away. When they got away from the mansion, Michael ripped Alexandra's hand away from his mouth.

"Get your filthy hands off of me!" Michael yelled.

"How dumb are you?" Alexandra asked.

"Excuse you!"

"Hey, before everyone starts arguing," Ji-yoon interrupted. "Where are we going?"

"Yeah, Alex, you never told me anything," Jazmine said.

Alex glanced around the area before motioning everyone to come closer. They looked at each other before doing so. Michael mumbled something under his breath as he joined in.

"We're going into the forbidden forest."

"Yep, you're the dumbest person I've met," Michael said.

"Sis, really?" Jazmine questioned.

"You know it's forbidden, right? It says it in the name," Davis pointed out.

"I got up early for this," Ji-yoon complained.

"Come on, guys, let's hear her out," Hua said.

"Hey! It's not only the best place to have a secret meeting but also a special place," Alexandra explained. She opened her bag to search for the journal. After a second of rummaging, she finally pulled out the book. Alexandra flipped through and landed on a page that showed the picture of the group of teenagers. She had taped it back into the spot that it was initially to help make sense of the journal.

"I feel that this is something that should shock us," Michael said casually.

Alexandra shot him a look before closing the book. She turned around and began walking in the forest's direction.

Everyone except Hua hesitated to follow her. The rest eventually followed Alexandra, with Ji-yoon complaining about her not dressing to be walking in the forest.

"I better not get kicked out of school for this," Michael said.

The forbidden forest was a few miles from the mansion and the school. It took them about two hours before making it to the forest fence. They could have made it to the forest earlier, but Ji-yoon had the group stop a few times since she was wearing heels. She did not plan to walk up a mountain to get to a forest. Hua did not have this problem since her brother was currently carrying her. Thankfully, there were no cars that drove past them. It would be hard for anything to explain why they were heading away from the school and city.

The forest was growing past the fence to where, if a person was not directly in front of it, one might believe there was no fence. There were no holes in the it, which surprised Alexandra. She was sure that at least one random animal would have messed it up. Alexandra grabbed and climbed over it but suddenly stopped. She turned around and pointed back to the road.

"Davis. Michael. Look that way."

"Neither one of us like you that way, especially me," Michael said. He and Davis, however, turned around. The other ladies climbed over the fence as well. When Hua finished, Jazmine nudged her.

"Are you sure that you should be out here in that short of a skirt? There's probably poison ivy everywhere."

"Or something can cut your legs up," Ji-yoon added.

"Look, sometimes we have to sacrifice ourselves for fashion."

"Whatever you say."

"Can we turn around now?" Davis asked.

"Oh yeah, you guys can jump the fence now."

While Davis and Michael jumped the fence, Alexandra scribbled down something on a blank piece of paper. Ji-yoon peeked over to see what her friend was doing. She figured Alexandra was trying to map out their travel. Alexandra started to walk deeper into the forest without warning the others. They chased after her, with Michael grumbling something under his breath.

Alexandra stopped when she found a small clearing big enough for the group to rest. She pulled a small blanket from her bag and placed it on a rock so her shorts would not get dirty. Alexandra scanned the journal again without telling the others what she was doing. Jazmine snatched the book from her hand and raised it above her head.

"We have been walking for hours," she started, "what was the point of taking us out here?"

"Yeah, couldn't we stay at your house? You know the place that has a heater," Davis said.

"Yeah, I waited to be in a mansion. I've never been in one before!" Michael exclaimed. "And it looked really nice based on the outside."

"I need all the details," Ji-yoon said as she took out her phone. "Just give me to pull up my notes app."

Alexandra got up and grabbed the journal back from Jazmine. She quickly flipped through it to get to the picture. Without warning, she tossed the journal back to her sister. Jazmine barely had enough time to catch it.

"I couldn't say anything because Ngo could have overheard me."

"It's not like he would understand what we're talking about," Jazmine said.

"Yes, he would, especially since he is in the picture."

Everyone gathered around Alexandra at that statement. Jazmine had looked at the picture multiple times, and each person had different photos across all the journals she had read so far, with some easier to recognize than others. She felt connected to some people but did not think she would miss something important about a loved one she knew. She scanned the picture, trying to figure out who Ngo was. If he was there, it explained why Jazmine felt connected to someone with the people in the picture.

Davis and Ji-yoon were curious about what Ngo looked like when he was younger. They see him often enough to realize he is not from this country. Sometimes, his accent would slip through, but he would quickly hide it. Ji-yoon tried to ask him once as someone from a different country, but he pretended he did not know what she was talking about. She tried to ask Alexandra and Jazmine about him, but they knew nothing about his past. Instead of changing the topic, Ngo would ignore Davis's questions about his life.

Hua did not understand the importance of why her friends' butler would be in an old photo. Ji-yoon had tried to explain what she knew about the journals Jazmine constantly read. She did not understand it fully since she was just told about it, but understood it was more important than anyone knew. Michael tilted his head, unimpressed at the revelation.

"I don't recognize the others, but I know for a fact that the man on the edge was Ngo when he was younger."

"How are you so sure?" Jazmine asked.

"He might be much younger in this photo but look. The guy in the photo has the same scar on his chin as Ngo, and if dyed his hair black, then it makes even more sense."

"But Ngo doesn't have a scar," Davis said.

"He does, but it's very faint on his chin," Alexandra explained.

"Wait, I thought these journals came from your dad's office? If Ngo is in the picture, shouldn't they be in his room or something?" Ji-yoon questioned. "It makes little sense for your dad to have it."

"I haven't figured that part out yet, but the flower in the journal is definitely my family's crest."

"Ngo has been working for our dad for a long time. Maybe Ngo asked him to keep them safe for him. It's obvious that a woman writes the journals," Jazmine pointed out.

"It is?" Davis questioned.

"Yeah, I've read plenty of these to figure it out. She's one of the girls in the picture."

She pointed at the woman that she felt the most connected to. She had the fewest number of pictures across the journals. The only time that Jazmine would see her was if she was sharing the photo with someone else. It made the most sense that she was the writer.

"What's the big deal that he's there?" Hua asked. "Does it mean something special?"

Alexandra stared at her. She opened her mouth, then slowly closed it. Jazmine could tell that every gear in her sister's head was turning. It did not seem like Alexandra thought that far about it. Ngo, being a part of the picture, was probably enough of a big deal for her, which Jazmine understood. Michael did not.

"You made me come out here in the winter for something that could have been a text?" Michael said. "I know it's weirdly warm to be in the mountains during winter, but I'm from LA. It's still too cold for me."

"Hey! I might not know his connection yet, but this is still a massive thing! And I think that this forest is connected to the journal."

"How so?" Ji-yoon asked.

"First, Jazmine, do you remember what was in the other journals?"

"Yeah. There were many descriptions of her adventures, and it was as if they were in another world. These amazing built archways, weird animals, and magic."

The group stared at the sisters. Ji-yoon closed her phone and placed it back in her purse. Davis and Hua looked at each other in disbelief before turning to Michael. He was swaying back and forward. They could tell that he was on the verge of exploding.

"Magic isn't real," he said slowly. "And what does this stupid forest have to do with anything?"

"I thought that too until I realized this forest is brought property," Alexandra explained. "And my father is the one who owns it."

"Wait, he does?" Jazmine question. "This isn't a place that would grab his attention."

"It wouldn't if there wasn't something important here."

"Like a flower," Davis realized. "Wait, a second. Is your family's flower the key to the cure for cancer?"

Alexandra and Jazmine looked at each other with shock and confusion. They had never made that connection. It was a stretch, but it made sense to them.

"I think so. He never told us how he made it, and no one has been able to make a copy of it either."

"Huh, I always thought the plant that would do that would be in the Amazon," Jazmine said. "And what would we do now with this information?"

"We're testing your hypothesis," Ji-yoon guessed. "We need to make sure that not only is this flower real but, also if it's really a part of the cure to cancer."

"If a flower like that exists, then maybe there is another cure that can be made from it," Alexandra said.

"Well then, time to get to searching," Jazmine said.

She started walking deeper into the forest without hesitation or waiting for the others. Davis and Ji-yoon looked at each other before following behind her. Michael was more accepting, following Jazmine, than Alexandra. Hua was about to go as well until she noticed Alexandra's face. Alexandra had bolted up from her seat with clenched fists.

"Hey! Wait a minute! You can't leave without me!" Alexandra yelled. "I'm in charge! I figured everything out till now!"

"And you did a fantastic job," Hua said to soothe her. Alexandra glared at her, which made Hua jump. She tried to say something else but ended up running towards the group. Hua was sure that she heard Alexandra curse about something under her breath.

Alexandra started walking with the group before they were out of eyesight. However, she kept her distance from them. Jazmine had the idea that if they kept walking straight, then eventually, they would find something. Alexandra pointed out that it was not the best idea, but everyone else was okay with her plan. It helped that not everyone believed they were going to find something.

"At least this way it will be easier to leave," Michael stated.

"Come on, it will be fun. And it's not every day that we are in the most secluded place in the area," Jazmine said.

"I'm surprised, Michael. I thought you would enjoy something like this," Davis said.

"LA doesn't have all of this. I would rather be Christmas shopping for you."

"For me?"

Michael hummed a yes before walking to the front of the group. Davis tried to say something else but caught Jazmine's gaze. She was walking backward and was grinning from ear to ear. Michael had to turn her around before she tripped over an errant root.

"Ah, young love," Ji-yoon said.

"Shut up."

The group continued to walk nonstop for over an hour. Ji-yoon wanted to take a break, and Alexandra did as well, but she would not admit it, especially in front of her sister and Michael. Michael had to point out that it would be better if they kept moving. The high altitude and the current season had already made it difficult for them to be outside for a prolonged period. If they stopped, it would cause them more problems.

Michael was not heartless about Ji-yoon's problems. He would take turns carrying her and his sister when they got tired. He offered Davis and Jazmine the same thing, but they declined. Jazmine had no problem walking miles in one go, while Davis was too embarrassed to think of doing such a thing. Michael would rather walk off a cliff before asking Alexandra.

Jazmine seemed to be the only person taking in the scenery. She noticed how all the flowers, which were oddly in bloom, swayed in the wind. She could see the cloudy sky through the trees. The crunching of leaves under her feet gave her joy. She knew it was silly to be happy about, but she never took a hike like this before. It was hard to tell that it was winter here. Everything looked like what she pictured a summer's day in one of her books. Amazing would not be enough to see what she thought about the place. There was something that she found unsettling.

"It's so quiet," she whispered.

"The animals are probably hibernating," Michael said.

"What lives up here, anyway?" Ji-yoon asked.

"Snakes," Hua answered.

"How do you know?"

Hua pointed at an enormous snake slithering past the group. The group froze at the sight of the animal. Suddenly, Michael darted off, away from the snake and the group. Hua knew her brother would react this way and was quick to follow him. The others hesitated because they did not want to spook that snake into attacking them. Jazmine grabbed Davis and Ji-yoon's hands and ran in the direction their friends went to. Since she was farther back in the group, Alexandra had to run twice as fast to catch up with everyone.

Michael was so busy running that he did not notice a small cliff coming up. He tried to stop himself, but since his sister was right behind him, he tipped over it. Instinctively, he grabbed Hua's hand, which also caused her to tumble down. The two fell a couple of feet down, causing scratches and tears on their clothes.

Jazmine did not hesitate, jumping off the cliff. She saw Michael and Hua fall over but thought the fall was not as bad as they made it seem. Since they were hanging on to her, Davis and Ji-yoon also had to jump over the cliff. Jazmine could brace herself for a better landing. The other two were not as graceful, but Davis and Ji-yoon were in far better condition than the Huang siblings.

Alexandra was the only one who did not go off the cliff. She peeked over the ridge to see everyone brushing themselves off. She looked farther into the crater everyone was in and noticed a pillar-like entrance in the distance. The snake was nowhere near her, so she took her time climbing down the cliff. It was difficult climbing down as the rocks were slippery with some type of liquid. Unfortunately, it had not rained in days, so she had to rule out water. When she made it down, Alexandra quickly cleaned her hands with wipes that were in her bag.

"Michael, what was that?" Ji-yoon asked.

"Snakes," he whispered.

"Huh, I didn't expect you to be afraid of those," Davis said.

"While I do want to make fun of Michael's fears," Alexandra interrupted, "Jazmine, didn't you say that you read about archways in some of the journals?"

"Yeah, why?"

"Well, if anyone of you would have looked before you leaped, then you have noticed that something a few yards away from us looks like an archway."

Alexandra pointed toward the archway. Jazmine visibly got excited at her sister's discovery. She began bouncing in place. Davis had to hold her so she would not start bouncing around the crater. Shocked, Michael and Ji-yoon could not believe Alexandra's claims. If they did, that would mean that they would have to accept that magic could also be real.

"I guess you're that leader then," Hua said.

"Yeah, I am."

"Don't get ahead of yourself," Michael said.

Alexandra glared at Michael before taking the lead. The walk to the structure seemed short because they knew where they were going. When they made it, everyone was in awe. Jazmine instantly recognized it as an archway she had seen in the journals.

"Yeah. This is definitely it."

Chapter 7

The Gateway

The archway stood in the middle of the crater, with nothing surrounding it. The clearing had no signs of life except for a dozen snake trails coming from the archway and the plants covering it. No one knew how fresh the tracks were, which did not ease some of their minds. Multicolored flowers covered it, and when the group came closer to it, the archway was more detailed than they thought.

Michael was the most hesitant about going near the archway because of the snake tracks. Davis had to console him because Hua was too busy staring at the archway. Even though she saw the structure first, Alexandra wanted to avoid going near it either. Jazmine and Ji-yoon were the opposite. Jazmine's natural desire for adventure and Ji-yoon's thirst for knowledge drew them towards the archway. They took a few steps forward before Alexandra grabbed them. She did not want them anywhere near it.

"Alex, what was the point of leading us here if we can't get a closer look at it?" Ji-yoon asked.

"You can't just go up to it," Alexandra scolded. "Jazmine, do you know anything about this thing?"

"This one particularly? No," she said. "Based on the ones I have read about, this was the one they were looking for, so later journals probably have information on it."

"So, there's a chance we're not discovering anything," Ji-yoon sighed.

While everyone was distracted, Hua walked up to the archway. She reached her hand out to touch it. Curious about the material of it, she did not expect what she saw. Whatever made the archway did not use stone, marble, or any other substance that arches usually consisted of. Instead, the structure was made from wood. The flowers that covered it grew straight out of the grain. Hua wondered if the arch somehow grew into this odd shape naturally.

Hua knew how to tell what type of tree depended on its bark, but this was different. The rough exterior was something she never felt before. There were no trees in the area that could compare to it. The flowers were odd as well. None seemed to be native to the area, yet they were flourishing. She wondered if it was because of the tree-like characteristics of the structure that made it possible.

"Hua, get away from there!" Alexandra yelled.

"Yeah, there might be snakes in it," Michael added.

Hua ignored their worries. She swept her hand over the flowers. The idea of them being poisonous did not scare her. She probably had bug bites she did not know about covering her legs, so a swollen hand meant nothing to her. She could see strange carvings in the wood as she brushed the flowers out of the way. When her hand moved crossed into the entryway, Hua saw it disappear. The others did not see her hand disappear but saw a rippling effect in the archway's open space. Michael snapped out of his fear and ran to his sister. He saw her missing hand and pulled her arm away from the archway.

"Be careful!"

The others came closer to make sure that Hua was all right. Hua did not seem to have any side effects from putting her hand in what they now knew was a portal. She wanted to put her hand in it again, but her brother stopped her from doing so.

"You're not putting your hand back in there."

"But nothing happened," she said. "Or at least I don't think anything did."

Everyone stood around gazing at the portal. If Hua had not put her hand through, they would have not realized that it was there. It was seen through, so it was easy to assume that nothing was there. No one knew what to do. Jazmine rocked back and front as she thought. Davis saw she was planning to do something.

"Jazzy, what are you thinking?"

"We came this far and found a portal to an unknown place. Why are we waiting here? We should run through it."

"No, we shouldn't," Alexandra said. "We should go home to regroup and read the journals written after the one that we have."

"That'll take too long. We're already here. There is no reason for us to wait," Jazmine complained.

"We don't know what's on the other side."

"We didn't know what was on this side of the fence, yet here we are. We can take a quick peek and then come back."

"No."

The sisters were at a standstill. Neither one would give up on their idea. Davis looked at both and sighed. He stood in front of them. He did not think that they would get physical, but he knew when they argued, it would be a long time before anything got resolved.

"Why don't we take a vote?" Davis asked. "There are more people here than the two of you. Plus, we have been walking for a long time. We need to rest before we decide on anything. Jazzy, you said that you brought snacks, right?"

Davis took a couple of steps back before sitting down. He patted the space beside him, indicating that everyone should sit down. Begrudgingly, everyone did as they were told and formed a circle. Alexandra and Jazmine sat on opposite sides of Davis, so they did not have to look at each other. Jazmine pulled out some snacks and water that she brought and passed them around to everyone.

"See, isn't this better?"

"I must admit I didn't have a picnic in the middle of a forest next to a portal on my holiday to-do list," Ji-yoon said.

"I can't believe that magic is real," Michael said. "If your guys' dad and butler knew about it, why haven't they said anything?"

"We could probably find out if we read the other journals," Alexandra said.

"You're acting like it's easy for me to get them."

"No fighting. Let's take a vote and see what everyone wants to do about this portal thing," Davis said. "All in favor of going through it to see it raise your hand."

Jazmine, Ji-yoon, and Hua raised their hands without hesitation, which did not surprise Alexandra. Davis and Michael surprised her by raising their hands. Alexandra usually thought of Davis as the sane one in his friendship with Jazmine. He was the one who usually pushed her to do things around school when it was necessary. Michael and Alexandra might hate each other, but she thought he would be against it based on his reaction to his sister putting her hand in the portal.

"Are you serious? Do any of you have a brain?" Alexandra asked. "We don't know what's on the other side."

"Well, Jazzy did point out how you didn't know what was over here but still made us follow you," Ji-yoon pointed out.

"Well… Michael, there are probably hundreds of snakes on the other side. You saw the trails."

"Yes, and I'm terrified."

"Then why did you vote yes?"

"Because you don't want to go," he answered.

Michael gave Alexandra a smug smile before getting up. Clenching her fist in anger, Alexandra watched as the others got up as well. Even though she agreed to have the vote, she did not like the idea that no one was listening to her. Hua lent out her hand to help Alexandra up from the sand, but Alexandra refused to accept the help. She got up herself and brushed off the sand from her shorts.

Everyone gathered around the archway to prepare themselves. While it was a five-to-one ratio, the act of going in made some nervous. Alexandra tapped her feet impatiently. If everyone wanted to go in, then one of them should go through the portal first, and she knew who it should be. She elbowed her sister.

"You're the one who wanted to go the most, right? Then do it."

"Yeah, you're right! Thanks for the pep talk."

Alexandra rolled her eyes at Jazmine's enthusiasm. Jazmine took a couple of steps back and took a deep breath. At full speed, she ran into the portal. Everyone watched as she disappeared into a rippling effect of nothingness. No one knew what to do at that point. Michael cautiously moved his hand towards the portal. Suddenly, Jazmine's head popped out, frightening him.

"You guys got to come to see this," she said before going back through the portal.

"Well, here goes nothing," Davis said before running in after her.

Ji-yoon had to push Alexandra into the portal before anyone else could go in. She did not trust her to not go in by herself. Alexandra would have stayed in the clearing and waited for them to come back if she had the choice. Michael and Hua grabbed each other's hands before walking into the portal. Hua could feel her brother shaking at the thought of the snakes that could be there.

"Don't worry, everything will be alright," she said.

"Of course, it will be," he said sarcastically.

Chapter 8

Eden

Natural beauty was the only thing that Jazmine could say about this new land. Trees as tall as skyscrapers with leaves that covered the sky. There were a few strays of sunlight that could peek through them. There was grass that came up to her knees and flowers that grew past that. Jazmine felt like she had walked into a fairytale. She could not call this a forest but a jungle.

One by one, the others came through the portal. The emotions that they showed ranged from amazement to shock. There was nothing that could prepare them for this new world. Everyone stood in front of the portal in silence. Jazmine bounced in place, and unlike last time, no one stopped her from running off. In fact, Davis and Hua ran out into the jungle with her. Michael had to snap out of his shocked state to chase after his

118

sister. Ji-yoon could not help but to take out her phone to take pictures of everything. She nudged Alexandra's side.

"Bet you're glad you came now, huh?" she asked.

"Shut up."

"Hey! Come look at this," Jazmine yelled from a few feet away.

Ji-yoon's curiosity got the better of her, and she ran off toward Jazmine's voice. Alexandra tried to stop her but could not grab her in time. She did not want to stray too far away from the portal. The jungle was so thick it would be hard for them to find their way back.

"Why do I feel like something bad is going to happen?" she groaned before speeding off to find her sister.

Jazmine climbed over a few tree roots to find another clearing not too far from the portal. The grass was much shorter compared to the area she just came from. It made it easier for Jazmine to see a cliff she could have fallen from if she paid attention to where she was running. She stood near the edge of a cliff that overlooked the surrounding area. Hearing the others coming, she took a few steps back to let the others see.

"What's going on?" Alexandra asked as she was the last person to make it to the cliff.

"Look."

Everyone gazed at the new land. Trees covered the land, but what caught everyone's attention was the massive tree in the middle of the jungle with some sort of mammoth size black object wrapped around the trunk. They could see tree houses built inside it, with what seemed to be a castle in the middle. There was something gargantuan surrounding the tree, but no one could make out what it was. Jazmine thought she saw a desert mile behind the tree, but it was too far away for her to be sure. There were instances of color other than green in the scenery due to flower meadows and trees with different colored leaves. It also looked like there were openings in the jungle, but no one could see what was in them.

There were no signs of cities or towns that they were used to within the jungle. However, they could tell there were signs of life away from the gigantic tree because of different smoke pillars rising over the canopy. The people here decided that villages were better to live in because of the countless amount of plant life.

"The smoke must be coming from bonfires or something," Michael guessed.

"We should head towards one," Jazmine said.

"Are you crazy? Do you know how far they could be from us?" Alexandra asked. "And even if we make it there, we do not know if they're friendly or not."

"They probably are. The other people that were found in the different portals were more or less nice," Jazmine explained.

"How are we going to get down now, anyway?" Ji-yoon asked.

"We aren't!" Alexandra yelled.

"I don't know why you're still trying. Nobody listens to you anyway," Michael said.

Jazmine tried to find a way down the cliff safely. Ji-yoon and Hua joined in on her search. They both were curious about the life found in the jungle. Not as enthused as them, Davis and Michael took in the scenery more. Alexandra complained to whoever would listen to her.

Jazmine found a small opening in a tree that somehow had steps in it. She explored the staircase. It was a spiral type of staircase that took her down the cliff. Whoever made it knew what they were doing because each step felt sturdy. Jazmine did not know how long ago it had been converted into a staircase but guessed it had been years. Taking a purple ribbon from her bag, she tied it around a low-hanging branch so they could find it later. She quickly ran back up the stairs to grab her friends.

"You'll never guess what I found," she said.

Jazmine darted back to the tree. The others hurried to follow her. Seeing a tree with a staircase carved into it surprised them. Hua studied the tree. She noticed strange symbols that matched the portal archway but could not study it more, for her brother was calling for her from down the stairs.

"Where should we go now?" Davis asked.

"Our best bet is going straight to that big tree," Ji-yoon said. "It got to be important to grow that big and have a castle in it."

"Yeah, in the journals, the woman would always try to go to the castle in whatever world she was in to talk to the royal family," Jazmine said.

"Jazzy, if you know more information like that, tell us upfront," Davis warned. "This shouldn't be the first time that you're mentioning royalty."

"But that would take the fun out of it."

"You're going to get us killed," Alexandra said.

"And you're being too negative," Jazmine said. "What's the worst that could happen? Now, the last one to the tree has to show the new students around the school next spring!"

"You can't give away a job I gave you!" Alexandra yelled.

Even though Jazmine ran ahead, Alexandra was sure that her sister heard her. She did not notice that the others had run after hearing the punishment. Ji-yoon had even taken off her shoes so that she could run faster. Alexandra rushed to keep up with the others when she realized she was alone. She got out of that job once. Alexandra was not trying to get trapped in it again.

Chapter 9

Departed

The group ran towards the tree for a few yards before stopping. They realized there was no point in running since the tree was miles away. The above-ground roots were also a problem since they had to climb over them. Jazmine had to help Hua get over some of them as she was not the best climber in the group.

Traveling to the new world had already taken its toll on some of them. Ji-yoon already had blisters on her feet from walking up the mountain and had to get Michael to carry her for some time. If Hua did not have a rash before, she was sure she did when she stepped through the tall grass. It felt like a miracle that she did not have any bug bites.

Jazmine looked up to see if she could see the main tree. Unfortunately, she could see nothing because of the other trees covering the skyline. It would be impossible to know how much farther they would have to go until they found a clearing somewhere.

"As long as we go straight, there should be no problems," Jazmine thought.

She watched as Michael tried to climb up one of the smaller trees. Michael wanted to climb a tree that seemed to reach the sky, but Hua warned her brother of the possibility of getting hurt. Listening to her worries, Michael went to a tree the size of one from their world instead. He pointed out that there could be fruit up there for them to eat when the little amount of food they had ran out.

"Maybe we should've waited," Davis said. "We don't have enough supplies to make it all the way to that tree. Odds are we're going to camp out, too."

"Oh, so now someone is going to listen to me," Alexandra said.

"But there was no way of knowing when we could come back," Jazmine pointed out. "Plus, we found the portal by chance. Unless Michael wants to see a snake again-"

"Nope!" Michael yelled on top of a tree. He had picked a few orangish-red fruits that were shaped like a pear before coming down.

"Then we had to do it now," Jazmine finished.

"I wonder what's out here," Hua said. She wanted to change the conversation to something less argumentative. She pulled out her phone and made a list of animals they could see in the area. "I haven't heard any birds since we've been here."

Michael looked at the tree he had climbed. "I didn't see any birds' nest up there either. Maybe they live in the bigger trees?"

Michael passed out the fruit he grabbed to everyone, but he ensured that Alexandra received the least. Hua managed to fit one of the pear-like fruits in her purse but handed the rest to Jazmine to put in her bag. Ji-yoon did the same thing but had Michael peel the outside layer of one of the fruits so that she could eat it without ruining her nails. Alexandra had refused to eat the fruit on the grounds that she did not eat strange food, but the others were sure that it was because Michael had picked the fruit. Jazmine took her sister's share since she thought the fruit tasted delicious.

"Too sweet," Davis complained as he took a bite of the fruit.

"Do bears live in jungles?" Ji-yoon asked. "Because I don't want to get mauled by one."

"Bears wouldn't live in this type of environment," Davis answered. "I think they do better in forests."

"Well, we came from a forest, so one could have walked in the portal like we did," Ji-yoon explained.

"We only saw snake trails going into the portal. Maybe the other animals came in first?" Hua wondered.

"Those snakes were born here," Jazmine said.

"And how would you know?" Alexandra asked.

"Besides us seeing an unnaturally large snake before going through the forest," Jazmine started. She pointed behind Michael and Davis. A pair of golden eyes clearly belonging to a snake focused on them. "The snakes here seem really territorial of the place, so bears would probably run away."

Hiss.

"Oh, hell no!" Michael yelled as he stood up.

The group watched as the height of the gaze grew taller. The snake made itself known with its colorful appearance. Never had anyone seen a snake with scales that shone like rubies and gold. Half of them were too afraid to move, while the other half could not form words to describe what they were seeing.

"I've never seen a snake that big before," Ji-yoon whispered.

"It's bigger than a house," Alexandra said.

Ji-yoon slowly took out her phone and took a picture of the snake. Unfortunately, she left the flash on. The snake's eyes dilated briefly before releasing a huge hiss at the group. Not wanting to make it angrier, everyone started running and splitting apart.

Jazmine, Alexandra, and Davis ran straight toward the direction of the main tree of the jungle. Ji-yoon, Michael, and Hua followed them until Hua tripped. The other two quickly scooped her up and started running again, but none of them could see the others because of the denseness of the jungle. They did not realize that they were drifting away from the direction of their goal and the rest of the group.

Davis noticed the other three were missing when he paused to catch his breath. He wanted to check on Michael because of his fear of snakes, but when he turned around, he could not find him. He grabbed Jazmine's arm and pulled her closer to himself.

"We lost them."

"What?"

"We lost the others! They somehow got separated from us!"

"You got to be kidding me," Alexandra said. She took a few steps forward and took a deep breath. "Ji-yoon! Hua! Can you hear me?"

Davis and Jazmine looked at each other before setting their gaze on Alexandra. Jazmine was the one to speak up.

"You know you didn't call Michael's name, right?"

"Huh? Oh yeah, Michael," Alexandra said in her regular speaking voice.

Jazmine rolled her eyes and handed Davis her bag. She walked over to one of the larger trees. After walking around, Jazmine tried her best to climb up it. Alexandra did not stop her sister from trying to climb the tree. Davis had to run and pull her off it. He had to lay on her to stop her from trying again.

"What are you doing?"

"Isn't it obvious? I'm trying to see if we're going the right way. As long as we head towards the tree in the center, we're bound to meet up with them again."

"That's if nobody gets eaten by a snake," Alexandra said. "We should head home."

"You worry too much," Jazmine said. She grabbed her bag from Davis and pointed straight. "Off we go."

Jazmine continued in the same direction that they had been going. Davis followed behind her, leaving Alexandra alone, which she could not stand. Yet again, she was being ignored by Jazmine. She was the oldest and found her plan the better one. Alexandra was sure that her sister was going to get herself killed. She ran in front of her to cut her and Davis off from going any further.

"We're going home right now."

Jazmine gave her a look. "No, we aren't."

"I am tired of you undermining my authority, Jazmine Victoria Lee. The three of us are going back through the portal to wait for the others to pass through."

"No, that's no fun. We're doing it my way."

Jazmine tried to sidestep her sister, but Alexandra blocked her again. Alexandra crossed her arms and pumped out her chest. Jazmine did not understand what her sister's problem was. She tried to walk past her again, but Alexandra pushed her back this time.

"I mean it, Jazmine."

"Alex, just because you're a year older than me doesn't mean you're the boss of me."

"Oh, yeah?" Alexandra stepped up to Jazmine.

While Alexandra was only a few inches taller than Jazmine, how she was built made Alexandra seem more intimidating. Before their fight could escalate, Davis stepped in between them. Alexandra glared at him. She tried to push him away, but Davis grabbed her hand before she could touch him.

"That's enough, both of you. Like it or not, Alexandra, Jazzy has a point. That snake messed with our sense of direction, so we no longer know where the portal is. And I don't like the

131

idea of leaving the place without the others, so the best form of action is to head towards the tree as planned."

"And what about the snakes?" Alexandra asked in a mocking tone. "They probably get us before we get there."

Davis's eyes narrowed at Alexandra's statement. "And they probably get us before we find our way back to the portal too. If we're lucky, we might find some non-hostile people to help us."

"Yeah, no need to worry," Jazmine said.

"Jazzy, try to read the room next time," Davis said before walking off.

Jazmine shrugged her shoulders before walking as well. She had already begun talking to Davis about a different subject. They left Alexandra alone again. Alexandra remained silent, but her gaze never left Jazmine. She followed behind them and never responded to anything Jazmine tried to say to her. Davis gave her a look, but she ignored it.

"So, you ready to go, Alex?"

"You have to be kidding me. Fine, get eaten, then see if I care," Alexandra grumbled.

She turned around and headed toward the direction where she hoped the portal would be. Davis noticed Alexandra was walking away and tried to call out for her. Again, Alexandra ignored him. Jazmine turned back to see her sister. Alexandra was sure that Jazmine had said something to her, but the sound of Jazmine's voice made her walk away faster.

Chapter 10

Lost

In a different area of the jungle, Ji-yoon was trying to catch her breath. The snake seemed to be long gone. She did not know when it had stopped chasing them, but they created a distance for them not to see the massive creature or any signs that it could appear soon. Since no one in the group had any water, they had to improvise with the fruit that Michael picked.

She tried to use her phone to see if there was a way to call the others. Unsurprisingly, there was no cell service. She even tried to climb to see if she could connect to something. When she failed to get a signal for her phone, Ji-yoon plopped herself down next to Michael, who was busy eating some fruit.

"Nothing. There's no way for me to call the others."

"So, what we're supposed to do now?" Michael asked. "There's no way to find the portal home from here."

"Do you think we keep heading towards the tree in the middle of the jungle?" Ji-yoon questioned. "Or try to find the others? We can't be too far from them, right?"

"But we might run into that snake again, and I don't want to see that thing again," Michael said. He looked over at his sister, who was in a deep trace about something. She held her hand against a tree and rubbed the bark. Michael slowly went up to her and tapped her shoulder. Hua jumped at the sudden contact.

"Oh, it's just you."

"Everything alright?" Michael asked. "You haven't said anything."

"Yeah, it's just...."

"Just what?"

"Aw, lay off of her, Michael," Ji-yoon said. "She's probably just worried about the others. With the closest civilization being meters away and a giant snake, which I guess there's more of just roaming the place, I'm worried about them, too."

"Yeah, and knowing Jazmine, she'll probably walk them off a cliff," Michael said.

"Like you did?"

"It was an accident and wasn't that far down."

Ji-yoon got up and walked next to the siblings. Then placed her hand on Hua's head. Hua did not react to her kind gesture. She removed her hand from the tree and stared at it.

"There is something off about this jungle," Hua said.

"Well yeah, there are giant snakes and trees everywhere," Michael replied.

"Not that. When we were coming down the cliff through that tree stairwell, I noticed strange writing on it."

"Writing?" the elder teens repeated in unison.

"Yeah. I know it might be from those people in the journal that Alexandra and Jazmine talked about, but what if it isn't?"

"Who else could it be besides them?" Michael questioned.

"I think the people from those villages have been up there before and maybe even through the portal before."

"Now you're trying to scare yourself. There's no way that's a possibility," Michael said.

"I don't know Michael," Ji-yoon said. "We saw those snake tracks on our side of the portal, and we saw an abnormal size snake back in the forest. Maybe someone came from this side to ours before."

"Why would they want to come to our world?"

"Maybe the same reason as us," Hua said. "Curiosity? We went into the portal knowing nothing."

"Well, maybe not all of us," Ji-yoon said. "Remember, Jazmine's been reading those journals for a while. She might not have gotten to this part, but she probably has a good idea of what's going on."

"She didn't realize her butler was in the picture, though," Michael said.

"You know she isn't much of a thinker."

"It doesn't matter what Jazmine knows about this world or any other," Hua said. "She isn't with us right now. But I think the best thing to do is to find one of those villages or at least something that is like their building."

"Sis, we don't know if those people are friendly."

137

"Well, if we think about it, they probably are since it seems like there are more journals in Alexandra and Jazmine's mansion," Ji-yoon said. "They clearly made it back alive because Mr. Ngo is still around."

"Well, I guess anywhere than here would be a good idea," Michael sighed. "I'll lead the way."

Michael took two steps before being pulled back by Ji-yoon. She placed her hands on her hips. Glaring at him up and down, she huffed.

"Who made you the leader?"

"I'm the oldest. Of course, I'm the leader. Now come on."

Michael power-walked in a random direction. Ji-yoon looked at Hua to see what she was going to do about her brother. Hua simply shrugged and began chasing after her brother. Sighing, Ji-yoon followed behind her. In her mind, who was leading did not matter because they did not know where they were heading, anyway.

Michael and Ji-yoon began talking about random topics on their walk. It was hard for anyone to keep track of time. The time that their phones showed was the same time it was before entering the portal. It made sense to them why they could not get any signal, but the time on their phone freezing worried Hua. She tried to bring up her concern to the others.

"You're worrying too much," Michael said.

"Yeah, our phones are probably like this because we broke it coming here. We can get it fixed when we get back," Ji-yoon added.

"But that's just it. I can use all my apps on it, but the time isn't moving even on the stopwatch," Hua added. "If it broke our phone, everything wouldn't work, not just the cell service and clock."

"Don't worry about it," Michael said.

"It's not a big deal," Ji-yoon said.

Hua huffed and stopped walking. Michael noticed first. He turned around and was about to say something to his sister until Hua pointed to a small pile of fruit cores and peels. He recognized it immediately.

"Then what about the fact that we have been walking around in circles?" Hua said.

"But that's impossible," Michael said. He walked up to the pile and began to look through it. It was like Hua said. This was the fruit that they had eaten earlier.

"How did we go into a circle? We were walking straight," Ji-yoon said.

"I told you it's this jungle," Hua said. "The way that everything works here isn't normal."

Hua crossed her arms with a sigh of victory. She was going to make sure that they took her more seriously. Even though she was the youngest, Hua believed she was just as capable as everyone gave her credit for.

"What are we supposed to do, then? We spent who knows long walking only to be in the same spot we started in," Ji-yoon said.

"Well, I think... uh," Michael stumbled. "If the jungle is not letting us move forward, how did we get to this point?"

"We walked. Just like we were doing," Ji-yoon said.

"Maybe that isn't enough," Hua said.

Hua gathered her thoughts before walking in the direction they were going. If her idea was correct, she should be able to go somewhere. It was not long until Michael grabbed her hand to stop her.

"Where do you think you're going?"

"I think I know where, and that could be enough," Hua explained.

Michael let go of her hand. He did not understand what his sister meant by that but believed she knew what she was doing. He would not admit it to her, but Michael was terrified of this place. If he could stay away from more snakes, he would be okay with wherever they end up.

Ji-yoon followed behind them both. She understood even less what was going on. As a logical person, this place itself should not exist. It would be a lie to say she was not excited about seeing what she could learn from here. Ji-yoon made sure to let Michael know that if she got tired, he had to carry her, which the football player answered with a nod.

Chapter 11

Desired Path

Hua and her group found themselves walking outside the loop

they had been in for some time. They occasionally stopped so that

Hua could study the plant life and so that Ji-yoon could take a

rest. Luckily for them, there had been no more sightings of

snakes.

The question of how they could travel with no trouble

still confused them. While Hua knew what was going on, she did

not understand how it was happening. Michael could see that she

was in deep thought about it. He gently placed his hand on her

head and began to violently rub it. Hua tried to stop him, but

Michael put her into a headlock. He continued to mess with her

hair.

"Stop! You're ruining my hair! Do you know how long it takes to do it?"

"Sis, I don't think putting your hair into pigtails takes long. Ouch!"

Hua took a bite out of Michael's arm. He jerked his arm away. It was not deep, but he could see small implants and saliva on his arm. Ji-yoon laughed at the siblings' antics.

"You bit me!"

"Yeah, and you put me into a headlock."

"What type of animal are you?" Michael asked. "Such savagery."

Hua rolled her eyes. She was about to walk again until Michael grabbed her hand. Ready to yell at him again, Hua noticed how serious he looked. Fiddling with the end of her skirt, she looked down at the ground.

"Ready to talk?" he asked.

"About what?"

"You're thinking about something," Michael said. "You know you can tell me anything. Now tell me what's wrong."

Hua tugged on her skirt again before raising her head. Catching her brother's eyes, she could feel his worry for her.

While it made her happy that he cared, she felt annoyed at the sight of his face. She thought he was pitying her for being younger. Not wanting to show her annoyance, Hua took a deep breath.

"This place knows what we're thinking."

"What do you mean by that? You think everything here is sentient?" Ji-yoon asked.

Michael turned towards a random red tulip-like flower. He gently petted it as if it was a dog. Ji-yoon and Hua watched as he did it. Ji-yoon slowly turned her head to look at Hua. Feeling Ji-yoon's stare, Hua spoke up.

"I don't mean like that."

"Oh yeah," Michael said. "I knew that."

"Then how is this place sentient?" Ji-yoon asked.

She wanted to move on from Michael's strange behavior. While trying not to be suspicious, Michael was still petting the flower. The girls tried to pretend that they were not seeing him do it out of the corner of their eyes.

"I don't know how to explain it, but Michael, did you know where you were going when we first started walking?"

"Nah, I was heading straight to see where it would take us."

"I think that's the problem. When we were first walking, we did it without a clear idea of where we wanted to go. But I have an idea of where I want to go, and that's why we haven't been going in circles."

"I get it now," Ji-yoon said. "As long as we have a destination in mind, we can move around without any problems."

"Now that you said that, the only thing I was thinking of was not wanting to walk into any snakes," Michael said. "That's probably why we have seen none since earlier. Well, continue the way then."

Hua nodded. She walked through a large log instead of trying to climb over the tree roots. Neither Ji-yoon nor Michael questioned where Hua was taking them. They thought Hua was aiming toward the enormous tree, as it was their first goal. It would be impossible to find the others in the jungle, especially at the revelation that the wilderness had a mind of its own.

Going to the tree crossed Hua's mind. However, it was not where she wanted to go. Hua could not get the strange lettering she found on the staircase tree out of her head. She needed to understand what it meant and know who wrote it. While selfish, Hua could not let this opportunity slip away. She expected the others to understand her reasoning, especially Ji-yoon.

Hua did not believe anyone from the picture Alexandra showed carved the message. There was no reason for anyone to write in this language. This meant that someone from this world made it all the way to the staircase. It would not be far-fetched to believe that someone also made it through the portal. If snakes could make their way through it, then a more intelligent being could have gone through as well.

Then this thought created even more questions for Hua. If someone made it through, it should be documented somewhere. Jazmine would be helpful in this situation. She was the only one who had knowledge about the other journals. The author probably mentioned the language of the world in the journal that Jazmine had or a prior one.

"What do the intelligent lifeforms even look like here?" Hua questioned.

"I haven't thought about it," Michael said. "They got to do well with all this heat and shade."

Surprised, Hua did not realize that she had said that part aloud. She was thankful that her early thoughts were not broadcast.

"Whatever they look like, they have to be smart enough to build structures like castles," Ji-yoon said. "They even made villages in different parts of the jungle."

"All without disturbing the surrounding area," Hua added.

Hua inspected her surroundings. While she would have loved to see the sky, the treetops covered the view. It made seeing harder for them, but thankfully, their eyes adjusted to the jungle's lack of light. Different flowers grew from the few spots of soil that remained free from the tree roots and fallen limbs.

The only way they could tell that something was alive in the jungle were the dozens of snakeskins lying around. It made Michael uneasy to see them. He could not look at it. Hua had to hold his hand and walk him past them. She gave his hand a small squeeze, which he returned. Hua glanced at him and then at Ji-yoon, who was busy taking pictures of the jungle.

"I can do this," she thought. Hua was sure she would prove that she wasn't some helpless child they thought she was.

Chapter 12

Details

Tapping her foot, Jazmine waited for Davis on top of an overgrown tree root. She watched as he desperately called out for her sister. Alexandra had been outside their line of sight for a while. She refused to go towards the tree and thought heading home would be the better choice. Davis was sure that Alexandra was cursing about Jazmine when she thought he could no longer hear her.

"She isn't coming back, Davis," Jazmine said.

Davis looked up at his friend. He could see how unbothered Jazmine was about Alexandra leaving them. He did not know why he thought she would show any type of emotion about the situation. Jazmine was rarely bothered about anything.

"You know we should go get her, right?"

"She'll be fine. What's the worst thing that could happen?"

"You mean besides being eaten by a snake, catching some disease from a plant, or injuring herself by tripping over one of these roots?"

Jazmine shrugged her shoulders nonchalantly. Davis could not tell if she thought Alexandra would be all right or if she did not care about the potential dangers that she could face. Pinching the bridge of his nose, Davis tried to talk sense into his friend again.

"She could die, Jazzy."

"Yeah, so can we," she replied. "So basically, everyone is on the same level."

"Maybe it would be safer if these two stayed away from each other for a while," Davis thought. "This fight is different."

"Well, except knowledge about this place, I guess," Jazmine continued without paying Davis any mind.

"What do you mean by that?" Davis asked.

Jazmine's eyes widened. She realized she had said too much, and Davis knew. Before Davis could repeat his question,

Jazmine jumped down from the tree root, away from Davis. She did not want him to yell at her.

"Jazmine!" Davis yelled.

He climbed over the overgrown root with ease. Jazmine was waiting for him with her hands clasped together as if begging for something. This made Davis angry because this showed that she was hiding something. Jazmine could only apologize for what she had done, but Davis wanted to know what she was hiding.

"Jazzy, I asked you earlier if you knew anything about this place, and you said nothing."

"Yeah."

"I'm going to ask again. Jazmine, do you know anything about this place that you haven't told anyone?"

"Yeah, but in my defense, I thought it would take away the fun if I said anything."

Jazmine gave him a big smile after her revelation as if she thought he would also be happy about it. Davis made a motion as if he was choking someone. The smile did not disappear from Jazmine's face but lowered slightly. She dug inside her bag and pulled out a journal. Davis thought it was the journal from earlier, but as he looked closer, it was a different one. The drawing covering it was different, as this one showed some plants he recognized from here and a giant snake wrapped around a tree.

"This isn't the journal that Alexandra gave back to you. How do you have another journal?"

"I was already done with the other one, so I borrowed the next one to read last night."

"Come here," Davis said.

Dragging her feet, Jazmine walked towards Davis. The two of them did not break eye contact. Jazmine was too afraid to do so. She could not tell what Davis was thinking. He showed no emotion in his face, let alone in his eyes. Davis grabbed Jazmine's left hand when she got close enough to him. Looking at it, he picked out her pointer finger and held onto it.

"Tell me everything you know, or I'll pull your finger back."

Jazmine remained quiet. Davis sighed and pulled Jazmine's finger back. She tried her best not to say anything. Even though her face clearly showed the pain that Davis was inflicting on her, Jazmine did not want to give in to him.

"It's not like I lied. I just withheld some stuff I knew," Jazmine squeaked.

This made Davis pull Jazmine's finger back even further. After a few seconds, she had to give up.

"Alright! Alright! I'll tell you everything I know about this place!"

"Thank you," Davis said as he let go of Jazmine's hand. "Now start."

Jazmine sighed before flipping through the journal until a page of a hand-drawn picture appeared. She showed Davis the image to let him study it. Davis immediately recognized it as the scenery of the jungle.

"So, they made it here," Davis said. He took the journal to inspect the drawing, making sure nothing smudged. Everything looked like what he saw except for the base of the giant tree. Whatever surrounded it was in a different position.

"We're in the jungle side of the world," Jazmine explained. "I don't know how it happened, but beyond the jungle is a mixture of a desert and rocky land. It's weird because it's perfectly even based on what I've read."

"Good thing we didn't get stuck in a desert. At least here we can find food and water."

"See! Everything isn't so bad."

Glaring, Davis handed the book back to Jazmine. She gave a nervous chuckle as she put the journal back in her bag. Instead of standing out in the open, they continued walking toward their original goal. Davis knew it was unsafe to let Alexandra go alone, but it would be even worse if the two sisters were near each other. He would rather deal with a giant snake than deal with both of them.

Plus, Jazmine had been more active since entering the jungle. Jazmine would accidentally hurt herself if he did not watch over her. Davis did not know what came over his friend, but Jazmine seemed happier.

"I'm still mad at you."

"Fair. But if I told you guys, I would've ruined that adventure. Just think how lame it would be if I said everything."

"We could've been more prepared. Don't you think these people in the journal had a plan coming into this world?"

Jazmine shrugged her shoulders. Davis was putting more logic in the adventure than Jazmine ever had. For a long time, she thought the tales written were made up and that her adoptive

father kept the journals because they belonged to a lost lover.

"This being their second world, I guess they already

knew what they were doing," she answered. "I don't really know,

honestly. A lot of parts in the journals are rubbed out for some

reason. I think someone didn't want some of the information

known."

Davis looked at her. There was no anger or annoyance

like before. Instead, he looked bewildered. Davis realized that

Jazmine honestly did not know what was going on. She read the

books, yes, but did not comprehend the dangers that the writer

went through. He wondered if the author even wrote about that or

if the journal just held general information that the writer knew

beforehand.

"I have so many questions."

"Me too, dude."

Chapter 13

Solo

Not knowing how long she had been walking, Alexandra decided against taking a break. She wanted to be far away from Jazmine. If Jazmine could not understand that what she says is the correct way, why try to persuade her otherwise? Alexandra was sure that her little sister would get what was coming for her soon.

"Maybe if I'm lucky, she'll get eaten or at least gets poisoned by some plant," she said.

Alexandra stopped the moment she said this. She looked around to see if anyone had heard her. Knowing that Davis would most likely continue walking with Jazmine toward the tree and others being lost somewhere, no one was around to listen to her statement. Alexandra smiled at the revelation. She continued to talk badly about her sister and others as she strolled through the jungle.

Alexandra finally took a break after discovering a lake during her hour-and-a-half walk. The water was clear, and there seemed to be no fish in it. She looked at her reflection in the water. A couple of scratches here and a few cuts there. It could have been worse. A good rest and a hearty meal would fix her exhaustion.

"I can come back and get Ji-yoon later. If I'm fortunate, then Michael will get eaten too," she laughed.

She decided this place was safe enough to stay longer than she should have. This was the first time she could see the sky in a while. While she usually was not a fan of the heat, the jungle was better than she thought it would be. However, this clearing in the wilderness was the best place she had been to so far. Alexandra could get a good look at the environment.

Alexandra had to admit that the plants looked beautiful without the shadows covering them. A few looked strange, but she did not know if it was because it came from here or her lack of knowledge about plants. Having Hua with her would have been helpful. She was the one with the green thumb.

There was no breeze coming through the trees, so Alexandra had to settle by putting her feet into the water to cool off. She ensured it was safe by dipping a large stick into it. When she pulled it out and saw it did not melt or show any other effect, Alexandra considered it safe enough to use.

Dipping her feet into the water, Alexandra shuddered at the coldness of it. She expected the heat of the sun would have made this water warmer. Alexandra could still feel herself melting into relaxation. She was about to doze off when she heard a rustling from the bushes not too far from her.

"Can't fall asleep yet. It's dangerous to do out in the open like this."

Alexandra was hesitant to wear her socks because her feet were still wet, but she did not want to walk back to the portal barefoot.

Rustle. Rustle. Rustle.

"Maybe wet socks aren't the worst thing ever," Alexandra thought.

She quickly put on her socks and shoes. Not wanting to see what made that noise, Alexandra headed back to where she thought the portal was. Then a thought made her stop.

"We didn't go past a lake," she thought. "I better not be lost."

The thought of being lost made Alexandra mad. If Jazmine or Michael were here, they would have tried to climb a tree to see where they were. She refused to do anything of that degree. It was too barbaric for her.

Alexandra did the only thing she could. She walked straight in a direction and hoped that she would find her way back to the staircase, or at least the cliff. Based on what she remembered from being on top of the ridge, there were no other elevated places except where they came in. If she found that, Alexandra was sure she could eventually find the staircase that led to the portal.

"This is a much better plan than simply hoping that someone would help them," she said to herself. "Honestly, Davis goes along with what Jazmine wants to do too often. He shouldn't be dumb enough to follow her. But seeing his taste in men, no wonder he's in that position."

Wondering how long it had been since she first came to the jungle, Alexandra looked at parts of the sky that she could see. The clear blue sky she saw while at the lake was replaced by a cloudy grey sky. It might connect the world to her world, but the weather was not in sync. It would not rain anytime soon back home, but it looked like a storm was brewing.

Alexandra did not know how bad storms could be in the jungle, but she did not want to find out. The pace that she was walking in quickened to speed walking. In the distance, Alexandra could see a shining wall. Thinking that it could be something she could use to help her, she ran towards it. When she got there, she wished she had gone in another direction.

The shiny wall turned out to be made of reptilian scales. Even though the jungle was warm, Alexandra thought the scales were made of ice because of how cold they felt. The wall moved the second that Alexandra touched it. It felt like a mini earthquake. The trees surrounding the wall collapsed, and Alexandra could not keep her footing, either.

"Don't tell me this is a snake."

She could not tell where the head or the tail was on the snake. The size of the snake was barely shorter than the trees. It was taller than the one that she had seen earlier. Panicking, Alexandra tried to run away, but what she guessed to be the tail swung around. Trees were smashed into smithereens, and the ground was being pulled up. Alexandra did not know what to do, so she braced herself to be crushed to death, but it never came.

Hiss.

"Huh?"

Alexandra looked up to see a coffin-shaped snake glaring down at her. The snake lowered its head to take a better look at Alexandra. It tilted its head as if it was thinking. The dilated eyes of the snake changed into what Alexandra saw as human-like. Alexandra did not know what came over her, but she knew this was her best chance of escaping.

"H-hello, Mr. or Miss Snake," Alexandra stuttered. "I'm trying to get home."

Hiss.

Another mini earthquake caused a giant hole to appear before Alexandra. She watched as the giant snake slithered inside the hole. As fast as the hole opened, it closed at the same speed as once the snake was inside. Alexandra did not know what to make of the situation.

"What is wrong with this place?"

She looked up and saw the tree staircase. Before she could move, the dead vegetation around her rebuilt itself. Flowers bloomed, and a fresh layer of pollen filled the air. Giant trees shot up to take the place of what the snake destroyed. Alexandra had to cover her head so the debris would not hurt her. Once everything settled down, Alexandra took a good at the area. It was as if the snake had never been there.

Alexandra snapped out of her shock and ran towards the staircase. She wanted nothing else to jump out at her. If she wanted to come back, she had to make a plan first.

Unknown to Alexandra, another snake was watching her from the trees. This lime-green snake was small enough to fit in someone's pocket. The eyes of this snake were similar to that of a black mamba, then changed into pupilless eyes. The snake then decomposed into a pile of purple hyacinth petals.

Chapter 14

Escapade

At times like these, Davis wondered why he became friends with Jazmine. She was the one who wanted to continue the journey to the massive tree that lay in the middle of jungle. Jazmine would instead go deeper into danger than try to find the others or go after her sister. However, Jazmine took her time going to their destination.

Jazmine was having fun playing with the overgrown flowers. Bouncing from flower to flower, Jazmine was doing gymnastics while in the air. Davis would be lying if he said it did not look fun.

The flowers Jazmine was jumping on looked like sunflowers but were the size of a small truck. Davis touched one flower Jazmine was not using. Shocked at the texture of it, the

163

flower felt soft enough to squish. Whenever Davis squeezed it, the flower would return to its normal shape.

"These are unreal," he said to himself.

Davis punched the sunflower just to watch it fix itself. He did it several times before realizing he was getting off task. They had to keep going if they wanted to get to the tree promptly.

Thud.

"Ow."

Davis turned around just in time to see Jazmine miss landing on a sunflower. He did not hide his laughter. Jazmine joined in, too. She dusted herself off, and it looked like she was about to jump on a sunflower again. Davis had to grab her hand before she could do it.

"That's enough. I want to get to the tree as quickly as possible," Davis said.

"What's the rush? I'm fine with taking some detours," Jazmine said. Davis gave her a look that made her change her tone. "Fine. We're probably halfway there, right?"

"I don't think so. It's hard to tell with no signs."

"Maybe we should climb a tree to see how much farther we have?"

"I know you aren't talking about the ones growing all the way up to the sky. I'm not climbing one of these trees. I've seen skyscrapers smaller than most of these trees."

Jazmine blinked.

"But the farthest you've been away from the city was to get to my house. So how have you seen any skyscrapers?"

"You know what I mean, Jazzy."

"I guess I do."

"Come on. Maybe we will get near a cliff so that we can see our progress."

Davis grabbed Jazmine's hand to drag her away from the sunflowers. They took a few steps before Davis stopped. Jazmine accidentally bumped into him because she wasn't expecting him to stop suddenly. She gave him a strange look.

Davis ignored her and looked around. There was someone there; he was sure of it. Davis's eyes fixed on something that was on the left side of them. Whatever was watching them was hiding well.

"What's wrong?" Jazmine asked quietly. "Do you see something?"

"I dunno. Let's run."

Jazmine did not have to be told twice. The two darted off. The idea of finding whatever was watching them did not seem wise. Even Jazmine, who valued the aspect of adventure, did not want to potentially have to fight a stalker.

In the bushes of the area that Davis was looking at, an emerald, green snake the size of a postcard slithered out. It tilted its head in confusion. The snake seemed surprised that Davis could sense that it was there. The human-like eyes disappeared as its body dissolved into petals of stock flowers.

Davis and Jazmine ran for about fifteen minutes before pausing. Davis had stopped sensing the presence a while ago but wanted to ensure he and Jazmine were far away from the area. He knew it was not the type of snake they had seen earlier because he would have seen it. However, this made him worry.

"What do you think you saw?" Jazmine asked.

"I didn't see anything, but I know something was there."

"Maybe it was an animal or something? I mean, we know snakes live here, but we have seen no other type of animal."

"You read the journals, so you should know better than me," Davis said.

Jazmine thought about what she knew. Since the journal that she currently had was with them just making it to the jungle, there was nothing for her to go on. Then she tried to think about the past journals. The only other world that the group from the journal had been to be the land of water and ice. They could not explore the land much because they were not ready to be there. The author compared it to being in Antarctica. They could not find any life since they had been there so briefly.

"I don't know, man. It could've been anything."

Davis sighed. He knew it was not Jazmine's fault. Based on what she said about the journals, there could have been more information, but someone scratched it out. It was as if someone did not want anyone else to find the secrets of the different worlds.

"Uh, Davis."

"Hm?"

Davis looked at Jazmine. Horrified, Jazmine pointed at what was behind him. He turned around to see a Venus Flytrap twice the size of himself. It was clearly inching closer to him.

"You gotta be kidding me."

The plant snapped its jaws at Davis. He barely dodged out of the way. When he did, he noticed how the Venus Flytrap was drooling some type of acidic liquid. It was powerful enough to kill the surrounding grass.

"Even the plants are trying to kill us!" Davis yelled.

"Maybe it thinks we're bugs?" Jazmine wondered.

Davis did not have the energy to run again. He had to think of a way to make sure neither he nor Jazmine became the plant's lunch. Scanning the area, he saw a large stick. Jazmine watched as Davis picked up the stick. She watched as he tried to hit the man-eating plant. Jazmine picked up a few rocks to join in on the action.

Davis swung the stick with all his might. The Venus Flytrap caught his attempt at an attack. It lifted Davis into the air as he was still holding onto the stick. He tried to kick the plant into letting his weapon go, but it refused.

Jazmine noticed how the Venus Flytrap had a tough time melting the stick. The plant spit it out once it realized the stick was not a food source. The damage to the stick astonished Davis. Even though it was having a tough time melting, the excess saliva on it continued the process. He had to throw the stick away because he was afraid that it would somehow end up on him.

Jazmine took this opportunity to throw rocks into its mouth. If it had a tough time melting the stick, then stones would be even harder. She had to time it perfectly. When the Venus Flytrap tried to snap its jaws at Davis again, Jazmine threw a few rocks into its mouth.

The overgrown plant had difficulty spitting the rocks out compared to the stick. Jazmine figured that since the rocks were smaller than the stick, it would take longer to fall out of its mouth.

"Isn't the mouth of these things sticky?" Davis asked.

"Yeah, I think so, to make sure bugs can't escape."

"Well then, let's fill this thing up."

Davis picked up some rocks and threw them inside the plant. He and Jazmine circled around the Venus Flytrap to get it confused. Even without facial expressions, they could tell that it was getting frustrated. It snapped randomly between the two of them.

They continued to circle it until the mixture of rocks weighed it down, and the confusion got the best of the Venus

Flytrap. The plant had a tough time moving its mouth. It tried to snap at Jazmine, but its body was too heavy for it to move correctly. It collapsed on the ground in front of her. After wiggling around, it stopped and accepted its defeat.

Davis walked over to Jazmine and gave her a high-five. The two of them laughed over their victory. They even gave peace signs to the plant.

They heard a rustle coming from under their feet as they walked away. Before they could react, a net scooped the two of them up. They dangled around twenty feet in the air. Jazmine could swear that she could hear the Venus Flytrap laughing below them.

"At least the branch doesn't look like it's going to break," Davis sighed.

"Yeah, what's the worst that could happen now?"

The second Jazmine said that Davis felt a raindrop hit his nose. He looked up, which was hard to do in his position, and felt a few more drops fall onto him. It did not take long before it rained heavily. The rain was strong enough to break through the top layer of trees to hit the ground.

"Well, at least nothing else could happen to us," Jazmine said.

Suddenly, they felt something jump onto the branch holding them up. They could see a person holding a spear with a giant snake wrapped around them a few feet away. The person was human in shape but not in body. Instead of skin, a layer of scales covered its body. Its clothing was just enough to cover its chest to the torso area. It had pupils like a snake that glanced down at the Venus Flytrap, then onto Jazmine and Davis.

The snake that was wrapped around the person uncoiled itself. Since she had a better view of it, Jazmine could see that the snake was twice the size of its owner. Its scales were gold and brown and not dull in the slightest.

"But at least now—"

"Jazmine."

"Yeah?"

"Shut up."

Chapter 15

Ruins

There was no way for Michael to tell how long they were walking, but it felt like hours. It did not help that it was unclear when they would reach their destination. Michael did not know where his sister was taking them. If she was taking them to the tree, then she would not be fidgeting so much. It was as if she was afraid of being discovered by either Michael or Ji-yoon.

Hua might not admit it, but Michael could tell how curious she was about the jungle. She always liked plants. Michael was sure that if their parents were not pushing her into a different career path, she would choose something related to plants. Even though they were miles away, their parents forbade her from joining the school's botany class.

Michael watched as his sister took in every aspect of the jungle. She would stop and study the non-exotic plants, even the soil, which caught her attention. Michael could not see the beauty in these things like her, but he was happy that she found joy in them.

He then turns his attention to Ji-yoon. She was not as hyped about plants and soil as Hua, but she was taking multiple pictures throughout their journey. Michael knew a barely charted place like this was a fun zone for someone like Ji-yoon. He excepted her and Jazmine to talk about their findings later.

"You know I wouldn't be surprised if the cure for cancer came from this place," Michael said. "I just don't understand how Jazzy's pops found this place if it was the butler in the picture."

"Maybe Mr. Ngo told him about this place?" Ji-yoon replied.

"But none of that explains how they knew what plant to use, unless someone taught them about the plants here," Hua pointed out. "What I want to know is how this place came to be? Somehow, the portal and the inhabitants here lived perfectly with nature. I must find out how they did it."

Michael hummed. He realized where she was taking them, or rather, where the jungle was taking them. Since Hua was leading, the jungle would send them to the place that would answer her questions. He did not know what would wait for them at the location, and this made him uneasy.

"Maybe when we get to wherever we're going, we can learn something," Ji-yoon said.

Michael caught Ji-yoon's eyes. She understood what was happening as well. It did not seem like she cared about Hua sidetracking the group. Michael was fairly sure that Ji-yoon would have done the same things as Hua, but she would not try to hide it.

"What are we even going to find?" Micheal wondered.

"That," Hua said.

Hua pushed past the weeds to find abandoned structures that only seemed to be held up by the plants that grew around them. Even from their distance, the group could tell that the buildings were not houses. Ji-yoon was about to rush towards the ruins until Michael grabbed her by the collars. Annoyed, Ji-yoon slapped Michael's hand off her.

"What?" she asked.

"You two can't just run into a place like this. Someone is going to get hurt."

"We'll be careful," Ji-yoon said.

"Hua," a voice called.

Hua did not react to their bickering, which surprised Michael. She led them down the hill towards the ruins. There was no clear path going down it, as it seemed like someone originally built everything in secrecy. It was also hard to see anything in the jungle because of the lack of light, but there was even less sunlight in this part of the jungle.

It was impossible to tell what the planet's inhabitants used the old structures for, even at close range. Moss and vines covered the outside walls. Ji-yoon used the flashlight part of her phone to illuminate the inside of some buildings. Oddly, each building they checked was completely empty.

There were some structures that were sealed off by doors without handles. Ji-yoon wondered how anyone could get into it. After picking a random closed building, she began to touch parts of the door as if a hidden switch existed. When that did not work, she tried touching spots around the door. Nothing happened. Ji-yoon kicked the door out of frustration, which she regretted immediately.

"Son of a---"

Instead of focusing on the ruins, Michael watched Hua's movements. He saw how his sister's energy changed when she saw the ruins. Hua ignored the first couple of structures. The deeper Hua went into the ruins, the darker it seemed.

"Hua!" Michael yelled.

No reaction. Ji-yoon ran up beside Michael as she noticed Hua's weird behavior.

"What's wrong with her?"

"I don't know."

The two of them continued to follow Hua for twenty minutes. It was unclear where she was walking towards, as everything looked the same. Ji-yoon called Hua's name to snap her out of the trance she was in. When she did not answer, Ji-yoon ran to her and grabbed her hand. Hua immediately yanked her hand back.

"What is wrong with you?" Ji-yoon asked.

Hua did not answer. Ji-yoon continued to try to get through to her friend. She tried to stop Hua from moving by standing in front of her. Hua sidestepped to get past Ji-yoon, but Ji-yoon would not stop standing in front of her. Ji-yoon was getting annoyed that Hua was not showing any emotions through this.

Michael watched as the girls went through what he saw as a fight. He knew he should break them up, but Michael promised himself he would never try to stop a girl from fighting again, even if it was a small one like this. As he watched the fight, Michael took notice of the floor. While it made sense for the floor to be made of grass since they were in a jungle, Michael noticed they were standing on leaves.

He noticed these leaves were not the same kind as the vines surrounding the ruins. Michael swiped some leaves away to see the ground. Instead of the ground being solid, it was boggy. Michael pressed his foot into the ground to look at his footprint. It appeared briefly before sinking deeper into the ground as if nothing was underneath it.

"Something isn't right," Michael thought.

Michael looked back at his sister and Ji-yoon. Now that he was looking at them closely, he could tell they were sinking into the ground. Instantly, Michael ran and yanked both of them

177

to the side. However, Michael could not move. The soft floor was already sinking under the ladies' weight, but Michael's weight was too much.

The floor's disintegration rate made Michael think someone made the floor out of quicksand instead of a weird type of mud. Before Ji-yoon could snap at him for grabbing her, she watched as Michael dropped down a hole. She had to make sure that Hua and herself were hugging against a wall as the hole grew into the size of an oversized truck.

Hua snapped out of her trance the moment that Michael fell. She looked around to find him. When she saw the large hole in the ground and Ji-yoon running towards it, Hua knew something was wrong.

"Michael!" Ji-yoon yelled.

"Oh, no."

Michael braced himself to hit the floor. Instead of hitting the floor, he landed on a stone staircase. He could feel all the air in his body leave his body on impact. Michael could not stop himself from rolling down the stairs. With each step, Michael could feel each bruise that he was gaining. It took three minutes before he made it to the bottom of the staircase.

Opening his eyes, Michael could see Ji-yoon and Hua above him. If he were to guess, the hole was about ten feet deep. How he did not die was beyond Michael's imagination. Michael tried to move his body but felt a sharp pain in his left leg. He was sure that he had broken it. Although feeling heavy, he could move his arms, which he was thankful for. He waved to the others to show that he was all right.

"Don't worry! We're coming down to help you!" Ji-yoon yelled.

Ji-yoon hurried to find a long enough vine that she and Hua could use to safely climb down. None of the vines in the area were close to the size that she needed.

"This place has giant trees and giant snakes, but when I want to find a vine long enough to use, I can't find any," she complained.

"Wait, what happened?" Hua asked. "How did my brother get down there, and when did we get this far into the ruins?"

"I think you were in a trance or something," Ji-yoon explained. "Now help me tie these vines together. I don't know what type of shape your brother is in."

"Right."

Hua went to grab the vine that was closest to her. She wanted to do anything that she could to help her brother. Touching the vine, a faint green glow appeared on Hua's hand. The vine suddenly grew ridiculously long and thicker than well. In awe, she watched as the vine went down the hole. When she lifted her hand off the vine, it stopped growing.

"How did that happen?" Ji-yoon asked.

"I don't know."

Hua looked at her hand. The green light had vanished. Touching the vine again, she wondered if something would happen. When nothing changed, her attention went back to her brother.

The vine was long enough for them to climb it without worry. Ji-yoon went down first, followed by Hua. There was little light in the underground staircase, which made descending it harder. The two used the wall to help them walk down the stairs. Hua noticed that there were carvings on the wall. If Michael was not hurt, then she would have stopped to examine them.

When they got to Michael, he had his eyes closed. If not for his chest rising and falling, they would have thought he died from his injuries. Even though they did not have any of the equipment to bandage him up, the girls did the best that they could. Hua tore a part of her skirt to tie around some cuts she found on Michael. Ji-yoon returned to the top to bring two pieces of wood she tied around Michael's leg with a vine. They slowly helped him get back on his feet.

"Thanks. I owe you guys," he said.

"Are you kidding? You saved us," Ji-yoon said.

"I don't know how all this happened," Hua started. She squeezed Michael's hand. "But thank you."

Michael gave her a small smile. He lifted his head to take in his surroundings. Ji-yoon noticed and brought out her phone. She turned on the flashlight. The three of them started to walk down the underground path.

Hua knew she felt carvings on the wall but did not expect so many. On both sides, strange symbols covered the walls. She recognized a few of them from the tree staircase.

"Look at that," Ji-yoon said.

She pointed her phone at a large mural that started where the symbols ended. The massive tree that they were initially aiming towards was there. They understood what the mural was describing as they walked further down the pathway.

How the tree's roots were drawn caught their attention. There were billions of roots underneath the tree. Connecting to every plant on this planet, the mural showed that roots were going into an archway like the one they entered.

"So, the jungle is sentient because the tree is sentient," Michael said.

"That tree is giving life to all the plants here and back on Earth or at least related to it," Ji-yoon said.

"I don't think it just goes there," Hua pointed out. "Look."

The roots did not enter just one archway, but a few others as well. They did not know if it was because someone drew the archways by memory, but they could tell that these were different. Besides the design of the archways being different, someone painted the other archways in a circle.

As the mural continued, the group saw a picture of a massive snake with green scales with different plants growing on it, and a metallic wolf with black rocks coming from its back.

Both creatures were looking at each other before turning away. The wolf was not in the rest of the mural, but the snake was.

The next part of the mural showed the snake traveling a desert wasteland until it got to the tree. The group noticed how there seemed to be smaller snakes coming out to plant hybrids. The snakes grew bigger as they got to the tree, but none came close to the size of their creator.

The plant-snake hybrid wrapped itself around the tree. The next few scenes showed the tree going through different changes. The first drawing was what the group recognized as the same setting they saw on the cliff. A powerful-looking tree that looked full of life. Next, the tree's leaves turned orange and fell off its branches. Drawn with no leaves in the next part, the group could still feel the strength coming from the tree, even if it was a drawing. Then the tree had pink flowers that Ji-yoon recognized as cherry blossoms. After the tree bloomed cherry blossoms, it went back to looking like the same tree in the first mural.

"Maybe this is why the time on our phone doesn't work," Ji-yoon said. "It's winter for us, but summer here."

"But does that mean this place's time behind or ahead of ours?" Michael questioned. "The time on our phones might not work because we're in another world. I don't think phone companies have cell towers here."

"That was the snake," Hua said.

"Huh?"

"The black thing we saw around the tree when we got here was the snake," she pointed out.

"I think you're right," Ji-yoon said. "But what happened to it? The snake drawn here looks healthy, but the thing we saw is completely black. I thought it was a weird-looking rock."

"Maybe there is another painting that explains it," Michael said.

"But there aren't any others," Hua pointed out.

The mural ended with the final picture of the tree, but the path continued. The group questioned if they should continue walking or go back. Michael's injuries were not getting any better. He was trying to not show it, but Ji-yoon and Hua could hear him breathing heavily.

"Maybe we should head back?" Hua questioned. "I know it would be hard, but Ji-yoon and I can carry you up the vine."

"No, I'll be fine. We can keep going."

"Plus, from what I could see in some of those buildings, there is no medicine or other medical supplies we can use," Ji-yoon said.

"So, you already looked through some of the ruins," Hua mumbled.

Hua tried her best to think about what she missed in her trance. Everything was blurry to her. The only thing she could remember was someone calling her name.

Hua.

Jumping, Hua let go of her brother. The sudden movement caused a sharp jolt of pain to move through his body. Ji-yoon quickly had to balance herself to ensure Michael would not fall. When she made sure that he would not fall and get hurt further, Hua had already gone further into the cave.

"Hey! At least let me shine some light down there!" Ji-yoon yelled.

"Don't bother yelling," Michael said. "I'm pretty sure she's back in that trance from earlier. Let's follow her to make sure nothing happens."

"Right."

Michael and Ji-yoon followed Hua for half an hour but still needed to figure out where she was going. The murals were long gone, so there was nothing that they could look at besides what was in front of them. At this point, Ji-yoon was sure the path would go on forever.

"Where do you think this path leads to?" Ji-yoon asked.

I am sorry to say, but you three humans will not go any further.

The voice snapped Hua out of her trance, but unlike last time, everyone heard the voice. Instinctively, she ran back to hide behind Michael.

"Who said that?" Ji-yoon asked.

"I-I don't know," Hua stuttered. "This voice is different from the one I heard earlier.

"Show yourself!" Michael said.

"Look behind you," the voice said.

Before anyone could turn around, everything went white.

***

Miles away from the ruins, Alexandra finally returned to the portal. The rain drenched her from head to toe. She tried to cover herself with her bag, but the storm nearly blew it away.

Not glancing back to where her friends and sister were, Alexandra did not hesitate to go through the portal. Even though she knew it was not supposed to rain back in her world, it surprised her how clear the sky was. She looked around her and saw everything as before she and the others left; even the sun still sat in the same place in the sky.

"My phone probably works now," Alexandra thought.

She pulled out her phone to check to see if it worked properly. Everything seemed in order, but something caught Alexandra's attention. The time on her phone only moved five minutes forward.

It had to be wrong, was her only thought. She was sure that she had spent hours in the jungle. Not wanting to overthink the insanity that she had just been through, Alexandra left the clearing.

"I can figure this out after a nap."

Chapter 16

Villagers

Hearing grumbling, Jazmine could tell that Davis was upset with their current situation and could not blame him for it. The snake woman, or at least she believed, dragged them through the mud. The person's voice was high-pitched, like a woman, but Jazmine did not know if that would be the case for their people.

Curiosity getting the better of her, Jazmine wanted to know more about the snake woman. She lifted her head up to get a better view of the woman. While walking through the jungle, the woman showed no problem with her pet snake being wrapped around her. Jazmine wondered how the woman could walk so well with a hundred-pound snake weighing her down.

"Where do you think she's taking us?" Jazmine asked.

"Probably to her hole," Davis answered.

"Hole?"

"Don't snakes live in holes?"

"I don't know. I'm not a zoologist."

"You have been *so* helpful during this journey, you know that?"

"Oh really? Thanks, man; I thought that not knowing anything would get us killed, but I am doing a decent job," Jazmine grinned.

Davis rolled his eyes. He should have known better than to be sarcastic. During their conversation, the snake partly uncoiled itself from its master. It raised its tail and slammed it down on Jazmine and Davis to keep them quiet.

"You could've just told us to keep it down," Jazmine mumbled.

The woman spoke something to them but stopped once she noticed that Jazmine and Davis were not adding anything to the conversation. She went back to conversing with her snake instead.

Davis could not shake the feeling that they both knew what he and Jazmine were saying. He tried to listen to their conversation. The woman and snake could understand each other.

From what he could hear, the woman was not hissing back at the snake. Instead, the language she used sounded well thought out. He knew it should not be surprising that life here had a language system since they had enough intelligence to make buildings.

"I'm gonna get sick, aren't I?" Jazmine asked.

"If you sneeze, turn the other way first."

***

After being dragged through the mud and rain for an hour and a half, Jazmine and Davis felt the rope that was pulling them being let go. They could smell different fragrances. Curious, Davis quickly picked up his head to find that the woman had taken them to part of the jungle with many hills. Davis could not see very well, but he was sure that there was something else there. He nudged Jazmine.

"Do you see something from your angle?" Davis asked.

"Let me see."

Jazmine was in a better position than Davis to see the new area without straining her neck. Through the mist from the rain, Jazmine could see that the woman had brought them to a village. There were other humanoid snakes, like the woman walking around with some of them with snakes as well. They used large leaves as umbrellas to keep themselves dry from the rain.

The area's people had dug into the hills to make them their homes. She could see different colored leaves and flowers draped around the hills. Knowing that she had seen smoke from some areas back on the cliff, Jazmine wondered where they had started the fire with so much vegetation around. She could see some light flickering from some hills, so she knew they had a way to start a fire that could not spread to other parts of the village. The inhabitants seemed to create their own perfumes and probably medicine based on the theory that the cure for cancer came from here.

From what Jazmine could see, there were large clay vases throughout the village. The vases stuck out from everything else. There was nothing that Jazmine saw during her journey through the jungle with the same properties as the vases.

Excitedly, a group of small children ran up to the woman and snake. They were jumping around and talking to them about something. The snake could understand them, which showed that whatever language they were speaking was mutual. One child looked over at Jazmine and Davis. If they could've waved at the child, they would have.

"Hello there," Jazmine greeted.

Even with the language barrier, a scream still meant that something scary was in front of them. Finally, the other children saw Jazmine and Davis and did the same thing. The woman tried to calm them down but did not know what she was doing. Even though it had its back to him, Davis was sure the snake was rolling its eyes.

"Can snakes roll their eyes?" Davis asked himself.

"It's alright. We aren't going to hurt you," Jazmine said. "We're just really muddy and probably gonna catch a cold."

The children's reaction to hearing Jazmine speak was worse than seeing her. They got louder, which brought the attention of the adults. People and snakes of different ages came out of the hills to see what was happening.

"Jazzy. You talking is scaring them more."

"No, I can fix this."

"For the love of everything pure, please stop talking."

"Humans?"

Jazmine and Davis raised their heads after hearing someone speaking in English. The crowd parted to let an old woman approach. Slithering past her, the woman's snake made it to Jazmine and Davis first. The snake had black scales, but a few of them were sky-blue in color. Even though they knew little about snakes, Jazmine and Davis were sure that snakes were supposed to blend into their way into their environment to some degree. The blue spots on the snake would give its position away. Then the snake shook its tail, which made a sound.

"It's some type of rattlesnake," Davis thought.

Before they could think about it any longer, the old woman made it to them. She carried a cane carved out of caramel-colored wood with red jewels decorating the top of it. The end of the cane was sharp, making Jazmine wonder how effective the cane was for walking. Slicing through the vine-made rope, she realized the purpose.

Jazmine and Davis had to help each other up. Being covered in mud, their clothes were much heavier than normal. They got a better look at the old woman. She was half their size and had her hair braided down to the floor. Unlike the woman who took them, the elder was covered entirely in leather and leaves.

"Humans," the old woman repeated.

She walked around Jazmine and Davis to get a good look at them. They could hear her mumbling something in her language. After a minute, the old woman stopped and stared at them. Jazmine was about to speak, but the woman cut her off by raising her cane.

"Your magic is similar to your predecessors," the woman slowly told Jazmine. She pointed her cane towards Davis. "And yours is exceedingly rare. I did not know that humans carry the capability to hold such power and honor."

"Thanks?" Davis replied.

"Predecessors?" Jazmine questioned.

The woman who had dragged them to the village whispered something to the old woman, which was brushed off. She tried to tell her something again but was met with a whack on the head. The old woman turned around and told the crowd something that made them return to what they were doing, except for the barely clothed woman and their snakes.

"I am Dahlia, the Elder of this village, and this is my other half, Locus," she greeted as she pointed to a large snake. "Please follow me and my granddaughter."

Not knowing what else to do, Jazmine and Davis followed. Davis noticed that whenever Dahlia spoke to them in English it was terribly slow. He guessed that while she knew the language, she did not have any way to practice it.

Davis looked around the village. Even though everyone seemingly went back to what they were doing, he could still see a few people staring at them. The villagers did not feel hostile, and Davis felt like he was still in Silver Valley because of it. The only thing he found out of the ordinary that he accepted in this world was that the people here were controlling the plants.

With a wave of their hands, Davis watched strange-looking vegetables shoot out of the ground after their seed was buried. The adults only had to wave their hands to make everything grow while their teenagers picked everything. If something grew too high to reach, the plant would lower itself so the product could be in the picking range.

The snakes lazed around and watched as the adults and teens did their work in the village. There were some snakes that humored the children and let them play with their tails. Davis could see that the number of snakes in the village doubled the number of people.

"I wonder if the snakes could do magic too."

While Davis was scooping out the village, Jazmine focused more on what Dahlia had said. Whatever magic Davis had was unique, but Dahlia compared her magic to her predecessors. Jazmine knew she meant her parents, but that was impossible. There was no way that the old woman would know about her adoptive father, so knowing her biological parents was even more unbelievable.

The only thing that Jazmine could accept was that one of the teens who came before them was one of her parents. She had always felt a connection with the playful woman in the picture. Still trying to accept it, Jazmine encountered another problem with this theory. How was Dahlia the only one who could speak English and know they were humans?

"Please come inside our home," Dahlia said.

Jazmine and Davis looked outside the home. Instead of being inside a hill, Dahlia and her granddaughter's home was inside a tree. There were different colored vines draping down from it. Touching the bark, Davis noticed it did not feel as rough as he thought it would be. As she walked in, Jazmine saw that there was a red ribbon tied around a lower tree branch but thought nothing of it.

Shocked, the inside of the tree was five times bigger than what Jazmine and Davis thought it would be. There was only one room, but large leaves helped divide some of the space. Davis guessed the bedrooms were behind the leaves and counted that the home had three bedrooms. They could see a small table off to the side that was covered with different roots and mushrooms. In the middle of the room was a fire, but when Davis looked closer at it, he noticed it had some ruby-colored rocks mixed into the wood.

"Talk about a treehouse," Davis joked.

"Rather sparse, don't you think?"

"You don't need a lot to live a happy life, children," Dahlia said. She tapped her granddaughter on the shoulder. "Introduce yourself."

"Thorn," she said before pointing at her snake. "This Dandelion."

"I'm Davis Brown, and this is my friend Jazmine Lee."

"Come sit down. You must be tired from what my granddaughter has put you through."

"We're covered in mud, ma'am," Davis pointed out.

"It's fine. A little mud hurt no one," the old woman said.

Jazmine looked down at herself and then at Davis. She could barely see their clothes. There was mud in their hair too, but the rain washed some of it off.

"But you humans can die if you stay like this, correct?"

Dalila tapped the ground with her staff. Locus nodded before slithering off. Shockingly, it came back with two sets of human clothing. Jazmine and Davis noticed it was old-fashioned compared to their clothes. Davis was sure he had seen pictures of his mother dressed in similar styles when she was young.

"So, humans have come here before," Davis said.

Dalila hummed a tune before calling Thorn over. She said something in her native tongue before ushering Thorn away. Davis watched as Thorn walked over to one room hidden by leaves. She pulled it back to show that there was a large hole. He did not know how deep the hole went. Dandelion slithered off Thorn to move a branch growing inside the tree. Water dripped down to fill the spot within minutes.

"How did that happen?" Davis asked. "Is that the rainwater, or is the tree connected to another water source?"

Dalila hummed something before answering Davis. He did not understand what she said but realized she probably did not know how to answer his question. Dalila pointed at the pool of water.

"You two may use it to clean yourselves."

Davis was about to comment that he and Jazmine could not use the bath simultaneously. Before he could, Jazmine spoke.

"You can go first. I have something to ask her," Jazmine said.

Davis noticed there was a lack of bounce in Jazmine's voice. This was probably the first time he saw her look serious. He expected her to be ecstatic about finding life out here or getting clean.

"Are you alright?" Davis asked.

"Yeah."

Knowing she was not about to explain herself further, Davis headed towards the pool. Thorn tried to go with him, but he told her not to through gesture. Thorn did not understand why Davis did not want her in the bath, but she accepted his wishes.

She went back to the kitchen area to make tea. Davis looked back at Jazmine before pulling the leaves in front of him.

Jazmine and Dalila sat in silence for a moment. Dalila could see that Jazmine had so many questions she wanted to ask. She smiled at Jazmine. She could see so much of Jazmine's parents in her.

"Child, ask the first question that comes to mind."

"Do you know who my parents are?"

Confused, Dalila's face changed. She did not expect that type of question.

"Do you not?"

Jazmine shook her head. Dalila waited until Thorn came over with the tea before she started her story. Knowing that things would get lost in translation, she poured a red liquid into her tea, changing it to purple. She took a slip out of it before handing it to Jazmine to drink. Hesitate, Jazmine drank the tea. The taste of the tea was something that Jazmine could not describe other than awful.

"Your mother hated it too."

Not understanding why, Jazmine thought she could better understand Dalila. The accent was still there, but her words were more transparent.

"Ah, your mother. She was such an excitable child, and based on what the plants tell me, you are too."

"Ok, not to get off topic, but you can talk to plants?"

"It is a gift that the people on this side of Terrora share."

"Terrora?"

"The land of vegetation and minerals. I believe you can guess which side we are on. We are the Alorian, the people of the snakes."

The curiosity of learning about this world would have to wait. Never in her wildest dreams did Jazmine think she could talk to someone about her parents. Her adoptive father never spoke about her or Alexandra's birth parents. Neither did Ngo. It hurt when a topic like that was taboo in her home.

"Can you tell me more about my parents first?"

"Of course. The two of them came to our world decades ago, along with their friends. It was my first time seeing a group of humans and a Shadetorian before. Neither race usually comes deep into the jungle. At the most, Shadetorian would go through

the portal at the Sacred Tree to be in the city."

"Wait, what's a Shadetorian?"

Dalila looked at Jazmine as if she was crazy.

"That is what your father is."

"Huh?"

"Yes, your father. Haven't you ever wondered where

your magic comes from?"

"So, I can use magic?"

"Yes. It should be easier for you to access than your

friend, as humans' magic will awaken randomly after being

influenced by one of the Royal worlds for a while. But I've never

met a mixed childlike yourself before. Yes, we are allowed to

have children outside our race, but for you to be part human is

unique."

Shocking would be an understatement about how

Jazmine felt. She was told she was not completely human, like it

was no big deal. Then it hit her that there were more portals, but it

seemed like the one to Earth was the only one that was separate.

Her father must have gone through the portal on his planet to

meet her mother.

"Wait, maybe this can help. Can you tell me if any of these people are my parents?"

She dug into her bag and pulled out the journal. Flipping through the pages, she found the picture of the teenagers. She handed it over to Dalila to look at.

Scanning it, she nodded. Jazmine could see a smile forming on the old woman's face.

"There goes your mother right there," she said. She pointed at the woman that Jazmine had been eyeing. "The one she is reaching over was her brother, if my memory serves me right."

"I have an uncle. Then what about these people? Do you know them?"

"Yes, these were her friends. I never met them, but I was told stories about them from your parents and uncle."

Tears swelling up, Jazmine placed the photo back inside the journal. This was the best thing that could happen to her. She wished Alexandra were here to hear this. When not in front of their adoptive father or Ngo, Alexandra was open about wanting to learn more about her heritage.

Then it hit her. The journals that she had been reading were probably her mother's. She had been connected with her for two years and never knew.

Jazmine wanted to ask another question, but her words wouldn't not come out. She was getting choked up. Dalila saw this and placed her hands on top of Jazmine's. While the palms of her hands did not have scales, they felt rough.

"It's alright. You and Davis can stay here tonight," she said. "And don't worry about telling your friend anything. My granddaughter already gave him his cup."

Jazmine looked over at the pool. The leaves covered him, but Jazmine could still see his silhouette. When Davis realized they knew he was eavesdropping, he went deeper into the water. Jazmine could feel their shared embarrassment from her seat. She had never cried before around him.

There were so many more questions that Jazmine had. Yet, she knew Dalila would not have all the answers. If what Dalila said was true about finding a Shadeatorian, then she could find the answers she needed at the Sacred Tree. Dalila knew a part of her parents' story, so someone in the capital should know another part of it. Until then, she would have to wait.

Chapter 17

Night Along the Trees

Jazmine could not believe how beautiful the sky looked at night. It was as if the rain had never happened. Instead of being a solid black, the sky was mixed with purple, which made the moon and stars shine brighter than the ones back home. She could hear some villagers and snakes rustling outside.

Thorn had created two hammocks out of vines for them to sleep in. Jazmine had watched Thorn used a mixture of magic and hand-crafting to make it faster. When Jazmine complimented her, impressed by how well woven that hammock was, Thorn blushed before hurrying off somewhere.

Dalila had already agreed to help them find a way to the city built on the giant tree. Based on her story, Oak City was built centuries ago. The royal family of this world made the city on the roots and had some elements of the other half of Terrora influenced by its design. The royal family had created their castle in the tree branches. Dalila believed they created the castle there to make it easier for them to watch over everyone.

It had been hours since then. Looking at the night sky, she raised her hand towards the moon to see if anything would happen. She thought about what other things Dahlia had told her about her father. If her father came from a world with an eternal night, it should happen to her during the night.

"She said that it would happen on its own," Davis yawned.

"You still up?"

"No, not really. Just talking in my sleep, that's all," he joked.

"Why do you think haven't shown signs of magic yet?" Jazmine asked. "Or why neither one of my guardians told me about it? Both were friends with my parents, though I don't know how my adoptive father plays into it, yet they told me nothing about them."

"I don't know why they didn't tell you, but I understand the feeling of not being whole. No matter how many books I read

206

or documentaries my mom has on it, I will never fully understand my Dominican heritage without my dad. All I know is that he and my mom met when my mom was on a missionary trip."

Jazmine rolled over to face him. Little moonlight was on him, but Jazmine could still see his outline. In deep thought, he was staring at the ceiling. It was rare that Jazmine would hear about Davis's father. Thinking back on it, the only thing she knew about him was that Davis's mother met him while she was a nurse for the Navy years ago.

"Do you think the others are alright?" Davis asked. "You know, Michael's group."

"They should be fine," she answered. Jazmine could tell that he was trying to change the subject.

"How can you be so sure about it?"

"Because why wouldn't I be? They are all smart in their own ways, so it shouldn't be easy not to die. And my sister is too stubborn to die."

Davis hummed as he thought about Jazmine's answer.

"Do you want to talk about anything?" Jazmine asked.

"Not tonight."

"I know I was never good at empathizing with people like you are, but you can talk to me whenever."

"Thanks, Jazzy; I appreciate your effort."

"Alright, goodnight."

"Goodnight."

Jazmine rolled over to her side. While she thought that the noisiness of the village would keep her up, Jazmine welcomed the sounds. It differed from the silence of the mansion. She watched the stars for a few more minutes before drifting off to sleep.

On the other hand, Davis could not fall asleep. He was sleepy a moment ago, but thinking about his father shook his tiredness away. He wanted Jazmine to find her biological parents. She deserves to find out where she came from. Davis wanted that for Alexandra as well. While he craved a father, he could never fully understand their situation. Davis did not know how long it took, but eventually, he joined Jazmine in a peaceful slumber.

ZZZ...

"Davis, we're not doing this tonight," Jazmine said. Davis's loud snoring had woke her up.

ZZZ...

Davis answered Jazmine with another loud snore.

Jazmine knew she was going to have a tough time falling asleep.

She decided to look through her mother's journal again to pass

the time and see if there was something that she had missed.

Knowing that she wrote the journals about her experiences in

magical worlds made Jazmine want to learn more.

July XX

I find it pointless to write the dates anymore when coming

into a new world since I never know what day it will be on Earth

when I get back. Anyhow. We are in a jungle today, just like XX

told us. He doesn't know much about the place except what he

read about it. I've been asking him to give me the book of

fairytales he read. I haven't found the book, so I wonder if it is

from his home country.

"The person she's talking about must've been my dad,"

Jazmine thought. He could not give her the book because it was

not real. It was a cover he made up to hide that he was not human.

Jazmine hoped that he her mother the truth before they got

together.

Chapter 18

Osmanthus

"Are you alive?"

Hua felt a small poke on her face. She tried to brush it off, but whatever it was kept poking her face. She already had a headache; someone poking her was not helping. Grumbling, she opened one of her eyes. A small pale white snake that could fit inside her palm stared at her. He stuck out his tongue before head-butting Hua.

"It's time to get up," the snake said in a squeaky voice.

Hua blinked.

"Are you talking to me?"

"You're in front of me, aren't you?"

Hua blinked again. After a moment of silence, she jumped up from her spot. This spooked the little snake into slithering back a few feet. She did not know if it was because she got up too fast or if it was an aftereffect of what happened underground, but her head was throbbing.

Looking around, she saw that Michael and Ji-yoon were still unconscious. She went towards her brother to wake him. Before she could, she saw that his leg had been properly taken care of. Whoever had done this had the training to make a proper splint. They were also nice enough to give them real blankets, not leaves, to keep them warm.

Inspecting the area, Hua noticed they were above ground in a building. It was in better condition than the others that they walked past. When she looked out the window, the rain came and went. She wondered if it had started when they were underground or unconscious.

Then she noticed it was darker than it was earlier. Hua did not want to believe it was nighttime because that would mean they had been out there for hours. If she did not make it back to her dorm in time to do her daily check-in with her parents, they would ground her.

The snake came up to her and tapped her ankle. Looking down at the snake, he tilted his head. Hua was sure that his eyes were shining.

"Wow, you're really tall," the snake said.

"Yeah, thanks."

The snake nodded before slithering over to Michael. The snake started to head-butt him to get him to wake up. Hua decided to wake Michael up herself instead. Knowing him, he would panic if he knew a snake had touched him. If Michael could sleep through a pep rally, he could sleep through a snake climbing him, anyway.

"Ji-yoon, wake up."

Ji-yoon mumbled something that Hua was sure was Korean. She turned around and brought her legs to her chest. Hua sighed.

"I forgot you were a heavy sleeper, too."

Since it was already nighttime, Hua decided to let the others sleep. She sat in between them and let the snake climb up her leg. He looked harmless to her. He tilted his head and stuck out his tongue.

"Are we not going to wake them up?"

"No. It's pretty late anyway, so I should get some sleep too."

"But you just woke up. Can't you stay up a little longer, big monster?"

"I guess I could. And I'm not a monster. My name is Hua, and I'm a human. What's your name?"

"I don't have one."

"Well, I'm going to call you Osmanthus."

"Osmanthus?"

"Yeah, it's the name of a flower. There are a lot of different flowers around here, so I thought it would make sense."

Hua placed the snake on her chest. He continued to ask her questions about random things. Not as bothered as she thought she would be, Hua answered Osmanthus to the best of her abilities. It felt strange to her. It seemed like Osmanthus knew as much about her.

Chapter 19

Curiosity

Thud.

Falling over the fence face first, Alexandra was closer to her mansion. She figured she could tell Ngo a lie about why she was coming home early. The biggest problem was coming up with a cover story about why she was dirty and covered with cuts. If she was lucky, she could sneak in before he saw her.

Alexandra was halfway down the road before she saw a familiar car drive up to her. It took her every ounce of nerve in her body not to run away. Ngo did not bother getting out of the vehicle. Instead, he rolled down the window. Alexandra expected him to be angry, but Ngo looked scared instead.

"Where are your sister and the others?"

"Still back in the forest."

"Did they not come back through the portal?"

"So, you know about the jungle?"

"Answer me. Did they go back through the portal?"

"No, sir. They wanted to stay for a little while longer."

Ngo sighed. He mumbled something under his breath before unlocking the car door. Alexandra expected him to open the door for her, but it looked like Ngo was not about to get out of the car.

"Hurry! We need to grab you and your sister's things."

Not understanding what was going on, Alexandra did as she was told. Ngo did a U-turn so fast that Alexandra almost fell out of her seat. She looked at him like he was crazy. He didn't even give her enough time to put on her seatbelt.

Alexandra wondered where all the police were. Ngo was going double the speed limit, which was even more dangerous as the roads in the mountains did not have any rails on them. If he had not cut a turn quickly enough, Ngo would have driven him and Alexandra off the cliff.

"Doesn't only one of your friends' parents live in the city?"

"Davis's mom works at the hospital."

"Just her?"

"Yes, why?"

Before Ngo could answer, Alexandra's phone rang. She looked at the ID and saw that her father was calling her. He had never called her on her cellphone before. It was usually through the video phone at home. Alexandra was going to answer the phone, but Ngo grabbed it before she could. Rolling down the window, Alexandra watched as her butler threw it out.

"What are you doing?"

"Alexandra."

Alexandra straightened up at the usage of her first name. He had never done that before.

"Whatever happens, do not come back here," Ngo said. "That goes for your sister and your friends as well. It will be at least a day before Steven can make it here himself. He might send someone if it is faster. I will see Davis's mother as soon as I can."

"What's going on? Dad isn't supposed to be back until after Christmas."

"That man is not your father and never will be. He is the man who took everything from you and Jazmine."

"How could you say that?"

Not answering the question, Ngo gripped the steering wheel. Alexandra could see that he was holding back some type of pain. Ngo hit the brakes when they made it back to the mansion. He stumbled out of the car and over to the front door. While Alexandra was mad that Ngo insulted her father, she could not bear to see the man that raised her in so much pain. Alexandra jumped out of the car and helped Ngo through the door.

"While I get the journals, get as much clothing and medical supplies as possible in a bag."

"So that was you in the photo with the other teenagers?" Alexandra asked.

Instantly, Ngo knew what picture she was talking about. Ngo's face softened at the thought of the picture. It darkened a few seconds after. He rushed off toward Logan's office to get the journals. Alexandra hesitated for a moment before running off to her room.

It took Alexandra fifteen minutes to get the things that she thought she needed. She stopped by her father's office on her way back to the front entrance. Ngo had emptied out the drawers. He had already put them into a large bag. Alexandra could tell by looking at it that it was heavy. Walking into the room, Alexandra saw that a bookcase was raised above the floor on the left side of the room.

"Jazmine would have lost it if she knew there was a hidden passage in the house," she thought.

Peeking in, Alexandra saw Ngo typing away on a giant computer. The only light source in the room came from the computer. Alexandra could read nothing that was on the screen. Even with straining her eyes, everything looked blurry. A few pictures popped up on the screen. Alexandra could tell from the blurry silhouette that the pictures were of her and the others.

"What is he doing?"

Trying to get a better look, Alexandra leaned too far in and fell into the room. Ngo snapped his head around. He let out a sigh when he saw it was Alexandra. Alexandra shyly waved before entering. When she did, Alexandra noticed a vine coming from Ngo's clothes. It would have been hard to see if it did not reach his neck and was going across the computer keys. She reached for her own neck unconsciously.

"Ngo. What's that on your neck?"

Ngo tried to touch his neck, but it was difficult for him to do so. The vine branched down his left arm and possibly more of his body. Alexandra could not see it coming out of his right sleeve, so she assumed it had not spread to that side yet. She looked up at him to answer, but he could not.

Ngo walked over to Alexandra and placed his hands on her shoulder. He gave her a weak smile that she could not read. Is the vine hurting him? Is it because he was holding a lifelong secret from her and Jazmine?

"Ngo."

"Don't worry, you'll be alright."

"What about you?"

"Just make sure that you and your sister are all right. If I manage to do everything right, the two of you and your friends can focus on having the time of your lives in the other universe. Now drink this."

Alexandra looked at the small glass bottle Ngo had pulled out of his pocket. The bottle had scarlet red liquid inside of it. It also had a phoenix topper that sealed the liquid. She took the bottle and drank it in one go.

"It's spicy."

"And give this to Jazmine once you see her."

Ngo handed over another bottle of mysterious liquid. Jazmine's bottle had something different in it. Instead of it being red, the drink was Tyrian purple and had glitter in it. Alexandra thought it reminded her of the night sky. A dragon topper sealed the liquid.

"I'll take the bags," Ngo said. "It's time for you to head back to the portal."

Chapter 20

The Morning After

Twisting and turning, Michael could not understand why his bed felt so tough. He tried to turn his legs, but something stopped him from moving one of them. Everything seemed off to him, especially the dream about him and the others in the jungle. Deciding that sleeping was not in his cards, Michael opened his eyes. The first thing he saw was not his alarm clock that was on his nightstand; instead, he locked eyes with a small white snake. Osmanthus stuck her tongue out as a greeting.

"Ahh!"

Michael tried to get away from the snake, but he had a tough time standing up. Since his leg was heavily injured the day before, he could not move it as he wanted. After walking on it without proper care, Michael's leg seemed to have worsened.

221

Ji-yoon and Hua had to rush over to his side to ensure that Michael would not get hurt even more. Osmanthus tilted his head in confusion. He was the only one who reacted that way towards her. It took them around five minutes to convince him Osmanthus would not eat him.

"Michael, your foot is longer than it," Ji-yoon said.

"Osmanthus is a girl," Hua corrected.

"Oh yeah, my bad."

Calmed down, Michael looked around. He had difficulty connecting where he was to what he knew to be true. It was not every day that you fell asleep in a jungle after going through a magical portal. He had to make sure that everything that had happened was real.

"Where am I?" Michael asked.

"We're still in ruins," Ji-yoon said. "Someone must've knocked us out to bring us back to the top."

"So, everything wasn't a dream?"

"Afraid not," Hua said.

"Shouldn't the broken leg tell you that this is real?" Ji-yoon asked.

"You guys did a good job patching my leg up."

222

"We didn't do it," Hua explained. "It was probably the person who kicked us out of the cave."

Hua helped her brother stand up along the wall. Osmanthus tried to slither her way toward Michael, but Hua stopped him from doing so. She picked the tiny snake up and walked to the other side of the room. Ji-yoon took her place by Michael's side.

Horrified, Michael watched as his sister talked to the snake. He did not understand how she could have a conversation with it. Ji-yoon got on her tiptoes to whisper into his ear.

"Ever since I've been up, she's been talking to her. She calls her Osmanthus," Ji-yoon explained.

"Since when could she speak snake?"

"Your guess is as good as mine."

***

The group took a stroll around the ruins after eating the last few squished fruits that Michael had on him. Michael claimed that moving around would help his leg. While still in immense pain, he moved around better because his leg was patched up correctly.

"So, what happened to the hole?" Michael asked. "Shouldn't we have seen it by now?"

"A hole that big should be easy to find," Ji-yoon said. "Maybe that person who took us filled it."

"Whatever the deal is, be careful. From experience, I can say that falling down is not fun."

Michael glanced over to Hua. She was busy talking to her new pet snake, which she swore she could speak to. The two of them were oddly connected. Michael guessed it had something to do with the jungle. Ji-yoon had told him earlier that the vine grew longer after his sister touched it. The jungle was influencing her.

"We should keep going towards the tree," Hua said. "If someone was with us in the ruins, then he possibly lived around here. Heading that way hasn't let us down yet."

"Well, there isn't anything else left to do here," Ji-yoon said.

"Ahh!"

Everyone turned their heads toward the source of the screaming. While it was hard to see the sky, they could swear that a person and their bags flew past them. The person landed in a field of roses that had so many thorns that it destroyed the beauty of the area. Since the field was near the ruins, the group saw the person land.

"So, are you going to ignore that?" Ji-yoon asked.

"I'm fine if we do," Michael replied.

"Wait! I think that was Alex!" Hua exclaimed.

"We definitely should ignore it then," Michael said.

Ji-yoon and Hua stared at Michael. They knew he meant that based on his lack of emotion. Ji-yoon sighed before heading north towards the rose field.

"Come on," Hua said before punching Michael's arm.

Michael winced in pain at the punch. Feeling bad, Hua patted where she punched him. She did not hit him hard, but in Michael's condition, anything could hurt him. Hua had to give Osmanthus to Ji-yoon so that she could help Michael out of the ruins. He refused to be near Osmanthus.

"Don't worry, he won't hurt you," Hua said. "See, he's harmless."

"You can never be too sure when it comes to this place. That thing appeared after we came above ground. For all we know, he was the one calling out for you earlier."

"But the voice I heard then was way lower," Hua said. "I don't know why, but I feel safe with Osmanthus. And this place gives me so much energy it's hard to explain."

"This place is your style," he said.

Giggling, Hua had to agree. This was the world of her dreams, besides the random danger. To her, plants are always honest.

Chapter 21

Roses

Alexandra has never been in this much pain in her life. From what she remembered before being thrown, Ngo said that as long as she had thoughts about Jazmine or the others, she would find them. What a lie that was.

The roses broke her fall better than she thought they would. The problem was that below the roses were its thorns. She had just gotten bandaged from the first time she came to the jungle. It would take her forever to pluck the thorns out of her back.

"That's if I ever get out of here," Alexandra thought.

The thorns tore through her clothes every time she tried to stand up. Alexandra could already see her newly gained cuts bleeding.

Alexandra thought about what she had done so wrong to get her into this situation. She was okay with wandering until she found someone. If what Ngo said was true, there should be no rush to find them. The jungle would lead them to her.

Instead, Ngo sped up the process. Alexandra had accepted that traveling to a different world was possible, but she drew the line at magic. She could not describe what Ngo did other than that. He went through the portal with her and waved his hand. A large gust of wind picked up Alexandra and blew her across the jungle. Because of Ngo's lack of aim, Alexandra would now have to think of a plan to get her out of this situation with the fewest injuries.

"How could this get worse?" Alexandra wondered.

"Alex!"

Alexandra recognized that voice as Hua. She sighed. It got worse.

Before Alexandra could yell out at her location, she felt something wrap around her stomach. At first, she felt the flower of the rose go across her, then its thorns danced on her body, slowly tearing at her clothes. Thankfully, it was not going deep enough to break her skin.

"Oh, come on."

***

Ji-yoon led the others to the rose field. It was even bigger than they realized. Ji-yoon knew she had landed in this general area. Alexandra would be close if they found the spot with crushed roses.

"Michael, you're the tallest," Ji-yoon said. "See if you can find where Alex landed."

Michael lazily scanned the area. Even though he was the tallest, it was not possible for him to look all the way to the back of the field. He knew that if he did not at least try to find Alexandra, he would get an ear full.

Suddenly, the ground shook. The roses shuffled around as if they were making room for something. The group took a few steps back as they watched something grow past the size of the regular roses.

"Guys," Hua said.

A monstrous rose bloomed from the ground. The lower part of the rose bent itself as if it was trying to see the three teenagers below it. They could see teeth in between the petals of the monster. Its stem had vines with thorns, which moved around like the monster was getting ready to attack.

In their fear and confusion, Osmanthus slithered back on Hua and wrapped herself around Hua's wrist.

"Found her," Michael said as he pointed to Alexandra, who was being held hostage. He did not have any distaste in his voice. There was fear placed in him at the sight of Alexandra being held ten feet in the air by the rose monster.

"Help!" Alexandra yelled.

"Don't worry, we'll get you down!" Hua yelled back. "Somehow."

Michael and Ji-yoon looked at each other. They did not know how they would set Alexandra free from the monster. If they weren't careful, they would be in the same situation as her.

The vines surrounding the monster slowly crept toward the group through the rose bushes. From the height she was at, Alexandra could tell something was wrong. She wanted to tell the others, but the monster placed one of the vines with a dozen thorns near her throat.

Darting out of the bush, a vine grabbed Michael's leg. If it was not for Hua stomping on it, Michael would have been taken away. The thorns had still left some marks on him. Michael thought it would hurt more since it attacked his good leg, but then realized that the pain from his other leg outweighed being stabbed by thorns.

"Michael, stay back!" Ji-yoon yelled. "You're too hurt to do anything without being in the way."

"Don't have to tell me twice."

Ji-yoon took the chance to gain the monster's attention so that Michael could find a hiding place. She ran towards the right side of the field and started waving her hands. The plant had no eyes but had to know where they were somehow.

"Over here, you overgrown weed!"

As the monster focused on Ji-yoon, Hua helped Michael get a safe distance away. She sat him down behind a tree before turning to leave. Before she could, Michael grabbed hold of her hand.

"Oh, hell no. You're not going back out there," he said.

"I have to. Ji-yoon will need my help to get Alex free," Hua explained.

"There is nothing you can do, and I'm not letting you get killed by that thing," Michael said. "We might not even be able to save her."

Hua balled up her fist. She could feel her face getting redder. He was downplaying her abilities again. Nothing was impossible. Alexandra was going to get saved, and she was going to help do it.

She did not understand how it happened, but Hua knew she had made the vine grow yesterday. She knew she could do something similar to the monster. The rose monster was just a plant, just like a vine. It could change sizes.

"Michael, I can do this," she said.

Michael knew he was fighting a losing battle. He knew how stubborn his sister could be sometimes. Unfortunately, Alexandra was her favorite subject to be stubborn about.

"If she doesn't thank you for this, I'm going to be pissed," Michael said. "You're thirteen. You better make it to fourteen."

Hua laughed as Michael let go of her hand. Before she ran off, Hua looked at him.

"It's like you said. This place is my style," Hua said. "If anyone could do something, it's me."

"I hope you're right," Michael thought.

Hua ran back to the battlefield to find Ji-yoon running around. Ji-yoon was doing her best to keep out of the monster's reach while keeping it entertained enough to not eat Alexandra. When she saw Hua had made it back, she smiled. She did not have the stamina to keep this going.

Raising her hands, Hua did not know what she was doing.

"Shrink!" she yelled.

Nothing happened.

Alexandra looked down at the situation going on below. She rolled her eyes at Hua's odd attempt to help. If it was that easy, then she would have done it herself.

Hua looked at her hands. She really thought that was going to work. Behind her, she could hear Michael sighing. He had said something after sighing, but Hua decided it was best to ignore him.

"Wait, when did I get this bracelet?"

"Maybe you have to touch it!" Ji-yoon yelled.

Before Hua could register Ji-yoon's recommendation, the vines from the rose monster shot up from the ground. It used its thorny vines as spikes and spears, which caused mobility issues for the girls. Hua and Ji-yoon barely had time to dodge some of the random attacks. If they moved out of the way of one long vine, they still risked being cut by the thorns.

Stepping on one of the spikes that barely were visible on the ground, Ji-yoon fell. Already tired by dodging its earlier attacks, she knew there was nothing she could do at this point. Ji-yoon looked at Hua to see that she was having a better time.

Hua had taken Ji-yoon's recommendation of trying to touch her new bracelet to see if a part of the plant would shrink. There was no reaction to the monster when she did touch it. Ji-yoon did not know if it was because Hua was barely touching it, because of the thorns, or if there was another way to do it. She did not remember hearing Hua telling the vine to grow yesterday.

How did she even do that yesterday?

Hua did not know how she dodged the monster's attacks so well. Like a second sense, she could feel where the vines would appear, even the shorter ones. She made her way up toward the monster. The rose field was the only thing in her way.

"Maybe if I touch the main part of it, then something will happen," Hua thought.

Alexandra watched as Ji-yoon and Hua failed to save her. She wondered if something had hurt Michael already, as he was nowhere to be found. Then it hit her. He would have to be forced to help if he was not injured. It would have been a mixture of not wanting to fight a giant monster and not wanting to help her. Alexandra felt annoyed by Michael's attitude.

She did not notice it, but the vine holding her was heating up. There was smoke coming from the vine that was not yet noticeable to the people on the ground. The monster let out a roar before dropping Alexandra back into the field. Thankfully, this time, she landed on her bags instead of directly on the ground.

"Ow."

"Did you do that?" Ji-yoon asked Hua.

"I don't think so," Hua said. She was not touching any part of the plant when it dropped Alexandra.

"That's enough," a voice said from above. "I can't allow you to burn this precious life."

Everyone looked up at the source of the voice. Floating in the air was a young man who seemed a few years older than

Michael. He looked almost human. As he drifted down to the ground, the group got a better look at him. The man had emerald green hair neatly parted down the middle that matched his green eyes. While it did not cover his whole body, some scales were mixed into his skin.

The clothing that he wore was something the group had never seen before. He wore a black-sleeved shirt with brown pants under a long teal coat. The coat looked expensive and handmade. There was a snake wrapping itself around his body, designed on his coat. As they approached him, Hua and Ji-yoon noticed the snake looked similar to the one they saw on the mural. On top of his head was a golden crown where a jade gem sat comfortably in the center. There was a staff that looked oddly like a king cobra in his left hand.

"What is with this place and snakes?" Alexandra wondered.

When the young man got to the ground, they could see that while he might be a few years older than Michael, he was nowhere close to Michael's height. Alexandra was sure that *she* was taller than him.

"On behalf of these humans, I do apologize for waking your slumber," the man said.

The rose monster mumbled something before shrinking itself and its vines down. After it was clear nothing else would happen, the teen slammed the bottom of his staff on the ground. Alexandra and Michael felt themselves being picked up from their spots. Large leaves were pushing them toward the rest of the group. The leaves placed the bags Alexandra brought with her next to her feet.

"Now then," the man started, "I have to figure out what I'm going to do with you five."

"Five?" Alexandra questioned.

The man pointed at the bracelet that Hua was wearing. It glowed a light green color before reverting into Osmanthus. Watching it slither around Hua's body, Alexandra backed away. She looked at the others, who looked more curious than surprised.

"You can turn him into a bracelet?" Hua asked.

Osmanthus tilted her head in confusion. The man laughed at the small snake's reaction. Suddenly, the staff he was holding glowed a muddy green before changing into a king cobra. It was bigger than any king cobra that could be found on Earth. It was

237

also more plant-like than any snake they had seen since being in the jungle.

"Creating your own companion and accessing the magic within you is difficult for a human."

"You can use magic too?" Alexandra asked.

"Too?" Michael questioned. "As in you, can you magic too, or do you know someone that can use it?"

"Bit of both," the man answered before Alexandra could. "Did you not know that?"

Before the man said anything else, the king cobra whispered something into his ear. The man seemed embarrassed at whatever he said to him. He rubbed the back of his head.

"My companion has made me aware that I haven't given my name," he said. "I am crown prince Akaibara. I rule over the jungle and all plant life throughout the universe."

"Nice to meet you," Michael said. "Now, back to you, Alex. Since when could you use magic?"

"I can't use magic," Alexandra answered. "If I could, I would've turned you into a toad."

"Your magic doesn't work like that," Akaibara said.

"Well, if I could use magic, I would turn you into the horse you look like!" Michael yelled.

"So, I'm being ignored?" Akaibara asked.

"You're talking a big game for a guy on crutches!"

"I am being ignored. Great," Akaribara sighed.

"Come on, guys, now isn't the time to fight," Hua said. "Your Highness, my name is Hua Huang, and this is my brother Michael and our friends Ji-yoon and Alexandra."

"Alexandra isn't my friend," Michael cut in.

"Quiet," Hua hushed.

"Sir, we aren't the only humans here. We have two more friends out in the jungle somewhere," Ji-yoon explained.

"Knowing Jazmine, she has probably gotten them eaten by a monster now," Alexandra said.

"Don't worry about your friends," Akaibara said. "They are currently safe in a village."

After the snake changed back into a staff, Akaibara held onto it. He closed his eyes for a minute before opening them.

"And it seems that they have already continued on their journey with help from the villagers."

"Wait, how do you know that?" Michael asked.

"I've been watching each of you since coming through the portal," he answered as if it was obvious. He did not understand why they were giving him strange looks.

"Why were you watching us? Do you have no type of morals?" Alexandra asked. She did not notice that the grass under her feet started to smoke.

"First off, lower your tone. Second, your group came into my domain and caused trouble by messing with life and accessing off-limits areas, even to my people. And third, I had to ensure that none of you would be a problem like the last batch of humans that came to the land."

"So, there were other humans?" Ji-yoon said.

"Who are you telling to lower their voice?" Alexandra asked.

"Lex, please," Ji-yoon hushed. "Sir, since you know where our other friends are, can you take us to them?"

"And can you give us some medical attention, please?" Hua asked. "My brother needs it the most after going through the jungle."

"Yeah, I was surprised nothing tried to eat us last night," Michael added.

"Last night?" Alexandra repeated.

"My plan was to take you all to the castle. Especially know that some of you have awakened your magical capabilities," Akaibara said. "I don't need your hotheaded friend here to accidentally burn down the jungle."

"I can use fire?" Alexandra asked.

With a swish of staff, the group felt themselves being lifted into the air. Akaibara had conjured rose petals to quickly transport them. They wondered how he could fly without the petals, but forgot to ask when they reached higher than the trees. Placing a sticky leaf on Alexandra's mouth before they flew off, Akaibara did not want to hear her until they made it to the castle. There was only so much he could handle. Michael could not be happier.

Chapter 22

Fast Travel

After a peaceful night with the security of the village elder

watching them, Jazmine and Davis were ready to head out toward

the city. Dalila was making Thorn, along with Dandelion, escort

them into Oak City. While they knew Jazmine and Davis were

harmless, people in the capital might not share the same idea.

As they waited for Thorn to finish getting ready, Jazmine

and Davis interacted with the locals. Davis tried his best to learn

the local language to gain more information about the village and

the surrounding area. He knew it would be hard to communicate

with them, but he did not think they would give so much free

stuff. Not wanting to be rude, Davis happily accepted the gifts.

Jazmine spent her time in the village playing with the

children. Unlike teenagers and adults, the children did not have their own snakes. The children could still control the smaller plants that were around the village. Watching a girl who looked around four years old make a flower spout out of the ground, Jazmine tried to do the same thing. She stretched her hand out and focused on the seed the children gave her. After a few minutes of trying, there was nothing different about the seed.

The little girl that was helping Jazmine patted her on the back. She said something to Jazmine before handing her the seed. Jazmine did not understand what the child said but got the gist of it. The child wanted her to practice with the seed while she was out of the village. As Jazmine continued playing with the children, Dalila walked up to them.

"It's about time for you to go," Dalila told Jazmine.

Excited that they would finally make it to their destination, Jazmine bounced her way toward Davis. She was sure the others would eventually find their way to it. Jazmine found no reason to be worried about them. Expressing this feeling at Davis, he sighed.

"Of course, you would think that."

"What? They're smart enough to figure out what they're doing," Jazmine said. "What's the worst thing that could happen?"

"Jazzy, what happened last time you said that?"

"Do you mean us being dragged through the mud or caught in the net?"

Davis rolled his eyes and went back to check the new things given to him.

"Just make sure you have everything," he said.

"Alright."

Dalila had given them some supplies to help them on their travels. Even though it would be easy to get to the city, thanks to Thorn, Dalila insisted that Jazmine and Davis had them. Besides giving them food and water in a handmade leaf canteen, she also gave Jazmine an elixir that she brewed. It had a grey, misty color with no smell. When asked what to do with it, Dalila told Jazmine to use it when she needed a good dream.

Dalila gave each of them a cloak to wear. It surprised them to see that fur covered the cloak. They did not know that there was an animal in the jungle that had fur. When asked about it, Dalila laughed.

"Don't worry about that right now," Dalila said. "I accept that you are not the types to want the adventure to be spoiled, or at least one of you doesn't."

"I do want an adventure full of mystery," Jazmine said.

"If this comes back to bite me, I'm going to be mad," Davis said.

"Time to go," Thorn interrupted.

Thorn had finished hooking Dandelion up to a wagon. It would have taken Jazmine and Davis days to make it to the city. Thanks to Dandelion guiding them, they would make it into the city within two days if nothing went wrong. Even if something attacked them, Thorn was capable enough to protect them.

"At the speed she drives, you will be there in no time," Dalila said. "Try to hold on."

"We will," Jazmine said.

"Wait, what do you mean?" Davis asked.

Dalila laughed before using vines to place them into the cart. The cart was the only thing that Jazmine and Davis could call normal. Made of wood, they recognized it as the style of how people used it in the past to travel. Thorn said something to

Dandelion as they settled down that made him dash off. Davis nearly fell out of the cart because of the snake's speed.

"I don't think we should go this fast when there's no road," Davis said.

"No." Thorn responded.

"She's really a woman of a few words," Jazmine commented.

Davis did not know if he should blame Thorn or Dandelion for their lack of safety. The cart would jump a few inches off the ground whenever it went over a large root. Davis was sure he heard one wheel coming undone due to it banging on the ground so much.

On the other hand, Jazmine was having the time of her life. Jazmine had never been on a carnival ride before, but she assumed this was what it was like. Hanging on the left front pillar of the cart, she tried to talk to Thorn. The young woman ignored Jazmine's yapping. This did not stop Jazmine from talking.

Davis wondered if Thorn could understand what Jazmine was saying or if the effects of the tea had worn off. Either way, they were in for a long trip.

***

Jazmine watched animated chrysanthemums the size of her hands bounce throughout the treetops. She figured that not every living plant would try to eat them, but seeing some of them be playful was interesting. Davis had warned her not to reach outside the wagon, but Jazmine wondered what the small creatures felt like.

It had been a few hours since they left the village. As Dalila said, Thorn was quickly getting them through the jungle. Davis crawled next to Jazmine. He was having a harder time with Thorn's driving.

"You, okay?" Jazmine asked.

"I'll be fine once we get on a proper road."

Jazmine began to rub Davis's back. Then, an idea formed in her head to get Davis's mind off the bumpy ride. Grinning, she turned to face her best friend.

"So, when are you going to ask out Michael?"

"Huh?"

"Yeah, it's obvious to everyone that you two like each other. Honestly, I don't know why he hasn't asked you out yet."

Jazmine watched as Davis failed to form words. He was waving his hands around in an attempt to explain what he was trying to say. This lasted for a minute before Davis managed to calm down.

"I have no idea what you're talking about."

"Davis."

"Michael is just my over-affectionate friend."

"That you like."

"I like all my friends, Jazzy. Now, I don't want to talk about this for the rest of the ride," he said.

Jazmine hummed. She did not understand why neither one tried to ask the other person out. From what she knew, there did not seem to be anyone trying to stop them from being together. If she was in their position, Jazmine was sure that she would be able to tell the other person that she liked them.

***

After a day and a half rollercoaster ride in the cart, Thorn had safely gotten Jazmine and Davis to the city entrance. Peaking from under the covers that Thorn gave them to sleep with, Jazmine looked at the entrance. She kicked Davis to grab his attention. This was different from what she thought it would look like.

"What is it?" Davis asked.

"We're going under the black thing we saw on the cliff."

"Snake," Thorn interrupted.

Being alone with her for over a day, Jazmine and Davis could learn a few words in Thorn's language. Thorn was not actively trying to teach them, so they had to figure it out on their own. While she rarely talked to them, Thorn was talkative with Dandelion.

The only words that they could understand were snake, sleep, and aristocratic. Aristocratic was the word that confused Jazmine and Davis. What type of conversation was she having to say that?

Davis thought he had learned the word for annoying. He wondered if that went along with aristocratic but decided it was not.

"She had to be talking about Jazzy," he thought.

"So, the big thing we saw when we first arrived was a big snake?" Jazmine wondered.

"I don't think it's still alive," Davis said. "Or at least I hope not."

The part of the snake they were going under looked like something elevated from the ground as if it had picked up part of its body for them. There were tracks leading through it, which showed that others had gone this way to get through the other side.

As they went under the snake, Davis touched its scales. It was warmer than he thought it would be. He thought it was because the jungle was naturally hot, but it did not feel right. There was something that he was missing.

"Is it still alive?" he wondered.

Chapter 23

Oak City

The city was something that Jazmine thought existed in fairytales. While she thought the city was just in the trees, it seemed it started from the ground, then worked its way up. Instead of being made of the environment like back in the village, they made the building out of stone. It also lacked the greenery that Jazmine knew from the land.

To make up for the lack of color, the residents used different colored stones to make their buildings. Jazmine wondered where they found the rocks. Even if the other side of the world was known for being mineral heavy, the quality of some of the blocks of stone was excellent. She was sure some of them used minerals such as emeralds and rubies.

While she saw the snake-like people walking around with their snakes, Jazmine was surprised to see another type of lifeform here. The best way she could describe them was werewolves, but at the same time, they did not look like what she expected. They were human looking mostly, but they had ears and tails like a dog. None wore shoes, and Jazmine was sure she saw some of them moving rocks around.

"Everything this rustic but shiny," she commented. "And there are people here that look different from the people in the village."

"Do you think the others have made it here?" Davis asked.

"I don't know. It would be pretty hard to know where the entrance is. For all we know, they could be walking around the snake trying to get past it."

"Maybe we should've explored around the snake before coming in."

"They'll be fine. You worry too much."

"And you don't worry enough, Jazzy."

Thorn took them a few blocks within the city before stopping in front of what appeared to be a saloon. She turned and pointed at Jazmine and Davis before pointing outside the cart. They quickly realized that she was telling them to get out.

"Where are we supposed to go?" Davis asked.

Thorn looked at him. Slowly blinking, she got off the cart and unhooked Dandelion. The two of them walked into the saloon without talking to Jazmine and Davis. After a moment, the teenagers realized they had been abandoned.

"Huh, I thought snakes didn't have eyelids," Jazmine said.

"Did she really leave us to go drinking?" Davis asked.

"I think so."

"How could she be so irresponsible? We don't even know how to speak the language."

"To be fair, I don't think she wanted to bring us here in the first place."

"Whatever, let's go somewhere."

Jazmine and Davis made sure that their hood covered their faces. Even if the city was more diverse than the village, they did not believe it would be a good idea to show their face. Humans were a rare occurrence here, and they wanted to avoid being studied.

Davis took the lead in walking. He was still determining where they were going, but anywhere seemed like a good idea at this point. He held Jazmine's hand as they walked through the city. Knowing her, she would get lost in an open area like this. Only a few days ago, Jazmine went to Silver Valley for the first time when she had lived outside it for years.

"She's the type to accidentally get run over by a car," Davis thought.

"Yo, Davis, look at that. The werewolves are wearing a lot of jewelry," Jazmine said. "Maybe they're the rich ones on this planet?"

"Well, it could be a part of their culture," Davis pointed out. "If the Alorian represents plant life, then they might represent rocks and soil. It's probably why the planet is the way it is."

"That makes sense, I guess. I wonder if those from the society of land of water and ice are the same way."

***

The two of them continued to walk through the city. Everything looked like a typical city besides the fact looked like it came out of a fairytale. Whenever they had to stop and take a break, Davis found a spot that was secluded enough that no one would bother them, but a place that still had people nearby just in case something was to happen. He did not know the area's crime rate, so he wanted to be careful. Currently, they were sitting in a park area, eating some food that Dalila had packed for them.

"Wonder why they have a park in the city right next to a jungle," Jazmine said.

"Well, we saw none of the werewolves in the jungle, so maybe they feel safer in the city," Davis said. "Either way, I don't think the Alorian would mind some more greenery."

"Do you think the fur on our cloaks came from them?" Jazmine asked. "It would be gross if they did. That would mean we're wearing someone's back hair or something."

"Nah, that would be immoral."

"This place has laws?"

"Jazzy, it's a civilization; of course, they do."

After eating their lunch, Davis allowed Jazmine to take the lead in exploring the city. He knew she would be less cautious in exploring the city than him. If the others had already made it to the city, Jazmine could probably find them. She had a talent for making things happen by accident.

The first thing that Jazmine did was find the nearest boutique. Davis gave the snake clerk a hello nod without revealing his face. Seeing a snake the size of him working at the cash register was strange. He knew the snakes here were more intelligent than the ones he was used to, but the snakes here performed multiple jobs.

Davis turned to Jazmine, who was putting clothes up to her body to see how they looked. The full-length mirror that Jazmine was using was decorated with a different animal that Davis hadn't yet seen on the planet. He recognized the winged animal as a Pegasus. It was holding up the mirror on its back. Davis noted the design as something to ask about later.

"I wonder if we're going to see any centaurs or winged centaurs."

"Davis, how does this look on me?"

"The first thing you wanted was do is go shopping?"

"If you wanted to find the others, wouldn't Ji-yoon and Hua be in a place like this?" she replied. "And you know Michael will not leave his sister to shop alone in a strange place."

"Carry on then."

Jazmine continued looking through the store's selection. Shaking his head, Davis wondered what was going on in his friend's head. Only she could find a loophole in wanting to do what she wanted. He respected that.

"We don't even have money to pay for anything."

"You're right," Jazmine sighed as she placed the dress that she was looking at back on the rack. "Where do you want to go next?"

Davis led her out of the store. Thankfully, the cashier was busy with a customer, so they did not have to interact with it. Davis was sure that if Michael was here, he would have a heart attack about seeing the number of snakes in one area.

"I think we should find some clues to see if Michael and the others have made it into the city," Davis said.

"But we got here because we had a ride. They're coming here on foot. I'd be surprised if they didn't get eaten by a plant or run over by a snake."

"Then do you think we should head back into the jungle? We agreed to aim for the tree, so they might have found a safe path to get here."

"I'm down with that, but do you remember which way the entrance was?"

Davis stopped. He hadn't keeping track of where they had been. At the most, he could find his way back to the park. He may have remembered how to get back there if he had not been angry when leaving the saloon.

"Well, if you don't remember where the entrance was, I know the perfect way to find it," Jazmine said.

"How?"

Jazmine pointed up towards the tree. To be exact, she was pointing at the castle built on the tree branches. It was the city's highest place, making it a perfect place to find the entrance.

Davis's eyes widened.

"You can't be serious."

"Come on, it's the best option we have. It's not like we can stop and ask for directions from anybody."

"Jazzy, we shouldn't be going anywhere near the castle. What if someone sees us?"

"Then they see us."

"Jazzy!"

"Just think about it. The royal family must have a special telescope to spy on their people, so all we have to do is sneak in."

"You want us to sneak in!" Davis yelled.

"Keep your voice down. People are looking at us."

Jazmine was right. Some citizens on the street were turning around to see what the fuss was about. They seemed confused as they realized that someone was not speaking their language. Quickly, Davis pulled Jazmine into an alleyway.

"Are you trying to get us killed?" he asked. "And how do you know they have something to watch over the citizens?"

"Why wouldn't they? Isn't that normal for any world power to spy on their citizens?"

"You gotta stop reading so many historical fiction books."

"But they're so good."

"Jazmine."

"What's the worst that could happen?"

"We are going to die."

"Come on, Davis."

"No, you don't understand. We will somehow make it there, and I bet you're going to mess it up somehow, which will cause us to be detained. After they see we are humans, they will either experiment on us or torture us. And that will be how we will die a slow and painful death."

Jazmine looked at her friend.

"You know, after all this is over, I think you should find a therapist."

Jazmine watched as Davis's right eye twitched. She finally recognized the situation that she had put herself in. Running as fast as she could, Jazmine headed in the castle's direction, or as she hoped it was. She could hear Davis's footsteps behind her and instances where he could not control his anger and was cursing at her. If he caught her, Jazmine knew he would never let her hear the end of it.

"At least he's following me towards the castle," she thought.

She had to twist and turn through the alleyways to ensure that Davis could still see her without being near her. The city's ground was leveled better than the jungle. It did not have nearly as many aboveground roots that they could have tripped over. This made the chase safer for the two of them.

There were times when she would bump into someone and nearly revealed herself, but Jazmine made sure that her hood never fell off. Jazmine was curious to know if Davis was having the same problem as her. If either of their hoods came off, there would be no chance of getting near the castle.

Chapter 24

Three Not of a Kind

Two hours.

It took them two hours to run to the base of the tree. Jazmine was thankful that they were already deep in the city before Davis chased after her. She looked over at her friend. He was just as tired as she was. It was customary for the sports teams at their school to make them do laps for an odd length of time, but this was the first time either of them had run this long without a break.

The two of them agreed to a truce. It was hard to stay angry when you were exhausted. They laid back against one of the roots to catch their breath. There were a few people in their area minding their own business. Jazmine did notice that there were more wolf people here.

"You're lucky that I'm too tired to fight you," Davis panted.

"You would not touch me."

"Yeah, I would've gotten Alexandra to do it whenever we saw her."

The two sat in silence for a while. Jazmine took the time to think about how they would make it to the castle. The castle was so high into the tree that it was impossible to see from her position. There was also a lack of soldiers at the base of the tree, which Jazmine thought was odd. She expected at least a few soldiers to be around even if the castle was miles above them.

Davis looked at Jazmine. They had been in Terrora for about three days, and something was bothering him.

"Do you want to talk, Jazmine?" Davis asked.

"What do you mean?"

"I mean that the two of you had a fight before Alexandra left. It was a few days ago. Don't you think you could've handled things differently?"

"You worry about things too much, Davis. She'll get over it and try to return to Terrora eventually. She's probably already traveling through the jungle."

Davis sighed. "Honestly, I don't know if this is a normal sibling thing or a normal *you* thing."

"A little of both."

The two of them looked up at the sky. The sun was setting, which gave the sky a beautiful orange color. This was their third nightfall in this strange world. They made it to their destination. The sacred tree caught their eye when they first saw it, but now Jazmine and Davis did not know what to do now that they were here.

Jazmine wanted to get into the castle but could not find a way to climb the tree. She knew that there had to be a way to get up there. While she assumed the Alorian used their magic to grow a plant that allowed them to access the castle, the wolf people could not do that. Jazmine had seen them move rocks before in the city. This could be how they did it, but she felt there had to be another way.

Davis saw how the wheels were turning in Jazmine's head. He knew whatever she was thinking was causing her to go in circles.

"Do you think that there're any inns that are free?" he asked, which caused Jazmine to come out of her thoughts. "We can't sleep outside."

"Not sure. It's not like we can ask them," Jazmine pointed out. "If we have to stay out here, at least we won't freeze."

"I guess that's the one good thing about being in the jungle."

"You know what I just realized?"

"What?"

"We haven't seen one bug since we have been here."

"And you're complaining about this? Why? You hate bugs the most out of anyone I've seen, Jazzy."

Jazmine looked at him with a blank face.

"I bet you that there's going to be a world full of them."

"No. No. Don't say that. Anything but that."

The two continued their conversation about the potential world and others. There was excitement at the possibilities that they shared. If the people on the other planets were like this, at least they would be intelligent. It also helped to place their fears about not finding their friends or getting into the castle in the back of their minds. Neither noticed that they fell asleep mid-conversation.

***

During their sleep, a loud rumbling woke them. They were sure that an earthquake was happening. When it ended, Jazmine pulled herself together faster than Davis. She quickly dragged him toward the source of the sound. Davis did not know if he was more confused about whether someone was making this much noise in the middle of the night or how energetic Jazmine was. He always thought that she was not a night person.

When they got to the source of the sound, they hid behind one of the tree's roots. Peeking over it, Jazmine could not believe what she saw. Three people were standing in a circle. She recognized one as a green-haired Alorian who wore fancier clothing than anyone else she had seen, and the one on his right side was a werewolf. This one showed a lot of skin as he was wearing a black crop top with black cargo shorts, his large tail hanging above it. He shared the same trait of not wearing shoes that the others did, but he had indigo hair, which she did not see anyone else have. She could barely see it from her distance, but Jazmine thought she could see multiple piercings in his ear.

The last one was a being she had not seen before nor had she read about in the journals. The person was tall but still shorter than the wolf hybrid. They had long scarlet hair that went to their back. Jazmine could not see their face clearly as the person's bangs covered the side of their face that was facing her. The new being wore a black trench coat with matching black pants and gloves. Jazmine would have mistaken them for a normal human if it was not for the large fox tail and ears.

"There's a fox person, too," Davis whispered. "I wonder what they can do."

"Hua talked about how foxes use fire in anime, so maybe that?"

"Really? I thought it was roses."

"We can ask her later."

Jazmine wanted to get closer to hear the conversation better but was afraid that one of them would see her.

Davis thought of using his phone to record the strangers' conversation. Thankfully, his phone was still nearly fully charged. He did not understand how, but decided it was best not to question it.

Davis chucked his phone into a bush after making sure that none of them were looking in his direction. This, unfortunately, caught their attention. The redhead stared towards the bush while the werewolf walked over to it. As he did, Jazmine and Davis saw that his right arm was a prosthetic. He sniffed around the bushes before shaking his head.

As the werewolf returned to his spot, the redhead fox began speaking. Based on the facial expressions of the other two, whatever they said was surprising. The Alorian continued the conversation and motioned towards the castle. As the conversation went on, the more agitated the werewolf became. He started to stomp around, which caused everything to shake. While the Alorian lost his footing, the fox did not seem affected.

"I guess we know who caused that earthquake," Davis said.

Jazmine pointed at the redhead. "Davis, look, that one is floating."

After taking a better look, Davis saw how their feet touched the ground again after the shaking stopped. He wondered how they could float like that.

"Could their magic have something to do with air? But wouldn't a bird with that magic be better?" Davis asked himself.

The fox said something before vanishing. The werewolf continued throwing his tantrum but without shaking the area. When he was finished, the Alorian snapped his fingers and told the werewolf to do something. Jazmine was sure that she saw the werewolf give the middle finger.

"It's good to see that is a universal thing," she thought.

The werewolf stood in front of the tree. He began moving the rocks around the tree using what appeared to be martial arts moves. A stone staircase that scaled the tree appeared in front of the werewolf. It went all the way towards the castle. The Alorian then made flowers appear on each step as if it helped keep the steps in place.

"I guess we know how we're getting up there now," Davis said.

"But I wonder where the other one went. Clearly, they didn't need the staircase to get up there."

Suddenly, a large rose bloomed around the Alorian. Jazmine thought it had eaten him but remembered Alorians controlled plant life. After a second, the rose squeezed itself and burst. Petals flew everywhere, and the Alorian was nowhere to be found.

The werewolf raised his foot. Jazmine and Davis readied themselves for another earthquake. Instead, the werewolf launched himself toward the castle, allowing the ground underneath him to pop up. Jazmine watched as a small explosion came from his prosthetic arm. She did not know if that was one of his powers or ability from his prosthetic. Either way, it helped him stay in the air longer.

"If they didn't need the staircase, why did they make it?" Jazmine wondered.

"I don't know, but I have to see if I cracked my phone by throwing it."

Davis ran to the bush. Pulling it out of the bush, his phone looked fine. The recording app was still working. He rewound it to see if it was close enough to pick up any part of the conversation.

"Here goes something."

"Wait a minute," Jazmine interrupted. "They wouldn't be speaking English since none of them are humans or come from an English-speaking place."

270

"So, I potentially almost broke my phone over nothing?"

"Well, it depends on what they said."

Playing the recording, it was just as Jazmine expected. The group was talking in another language. They kept listening to it, hoping to hear something they'd recognize. The words seemed complex and they guessed the words were common, but that they did not know them. Just as the recording seemed useless, a word that they knew came up, and they did not know how to take it.

Humans.

Someone had mentioned humans. Jazmine and Davis looked at each other.

"Do you think they meant us?" Jazmine asked.

"I don't know, but I'm starting to think that the others are already in the city, or rather, in the castle."

"But how? There's no way they can cause more trouble than we can."

"Well, do you remember the strange feeling I had a few days ago?"

"Strange feeling?"

"Yeah, it felt like someone was watching us. What if that person was watching the others, too?"

"And they didn't realize it, unlike you."

"And if they managed to take three people at once, it would be easy to kidnap someone who was alone."

"Alex," Jazmine whispered. Jazmine's eyes widened with horror. There was a big possibility that Alexandra was kidnapped before making it back to the portal. "Well, there's only one way to determine if the others were taken."

Davis looked at the stairs.

"If we hurry, we can reach the top before sunrise."

"Race you to the top."

"You were doing so well. Why can't you stay serious for more than a second?"

Jazmine grinned before taking off up the stairs. Davis wanted to get mad but knew that there was no point. She was going to see the fun of things, no matter what. If he was being honest, it was the best part about her.

"She's definitely going to get us killed one of these days."

Chapter 25

Break In

As Davis pondered their situation, the two of them climbed the staircase before the sun rose. They were currently hiding behind a pillar that was outside the castle. The posts and the castle's outer wall were made of smooth red and yellow stones. It seemed like the vines wrapped over the pillars were a stylistic choice rather than a natural occurrence.

From what they could see, the castle was made of an unknown type of tree bark. Neither would know what type of wood it was since Hua was not there with them. They did not realize how close the castle was to the end, but the outer wall went all the way out to the edge of the branch.

"They did a good job making use of the tree's big branches," Jazmine said. "It must've been a pain to get everything up here, though."

Looking up at the sky, Davis wondered how long the night lasted in this world. Even in the village, it felt that he had a full night's sleep before the sun was up.

"It feels like the sun is never coming up," he said.

"Huh?"

Jazmine looked up at the moon. After staring at it for a minute, Jazmine felt she understood how long the moon would be up for.

"Give it about an hour and a half; then the sun should be rising."

"How did you figure that?" Davis asked.

"Just a hunch."

Davis did not push the subject. Instead, he tried to find a way to get over the wall. Scaling the wall was possible, but he did not know what would wait on the other side. As it was still nighttime, he hoped most people would be within the castle.

"We can use the indents on the wall to climb over on the other side," Davis said.

"Then let's get to it."

Before Jazmine could climb the wall, Davis grabbed her by the back of her shirt. He shook his head.

"Even though we're climbing the wall, we have to find a good spot to do it. We can't go through the front, or we'll be seen."

"Then lead the way."

"Give me a minute," he said. "I want to scout out a good place for us. If I'm lucky, there will be a place where we can walk straight in."

Davis quickly hugged Jazmine before rushing off to the right side of the wall. The only way he would find a way in was by getting higher in the tree. He was not as great a climber as Jazmine or Michael, but he had to try.

After scouting the area for twenty minutes, Davis found the perfect place to climb the wall. It was on the right side of the castle, within the tree. The leaves in this area were thick enough to hide behind. The tree branch he was on was elevated enough for Davis to see over the wall.

Davis quickly ran back to Jazmine. She had moved from hiding behind the pillar to sitting on the top staircase. Waiting for the sunrise, she turned when she heard Davis's footsteps.

"Why aren't you hiding? Someone could've seen you," Davis scolded.

"It's fine. I would've heard someone coming up the steps, and the gate must open before someone comes out first. I would've had plenty of time to hide. Plus, the people who would walk around here are asleep or guarding the inside."

Davis rolled his eyes. There was nothing wrong with her statement. Besides the people from earlier, almost everyone was still asleep. There were Alorian guards on the inside station at specific points outside.

"It doesn't seem like guards move around much, so it should be easy to sneak through an unguarded door," Davis said.

"Or, if necessary, a window."

"Yes, only if it's necessary," Davis sighed.

"Then let's do this!"

Davis took them back to the area in the tree where they would climb the wall. If Jazmine's guess about when the sun will come up was correct, they had little time to sneak in before more people woke up. He let Jazmine climb the wall first as he watched

for any guards by staying behind the leaves. When Jazmine made

it over safely, Davis made his way over the wall.

Jazmine was in awe at the beauty of the exterior of the

castle. Even though it was created on a broad tree branch,

different flowers were growing from it. It ranged from red

flowers with yellow trim with sharp petals, which gave off heat,

and yellow flowers with white trim that seemed to glow. This one

had petals that were even sharper than the other flowers. Looking

closer at it, Jazmine noticed that static was coming from the

flower bulb.

There was a peculiar flower that caught her eye. It was

black with purple spots on its petals, which appeared to be closing

on itself. Next to it, Jazmine noticed that the pearly white flowers

were blooming at the same speed the other flower was closing. It

was odd. Jazmine felt like one was going to sleep while the other

was waking up.

Turning towards Davis, Jazmine saw he was studying a

particular type of flower. The flowers he was looking at were

unique compared to the others, as they did not have a set color.

Each flower in that section was switching throughout all the colors to its own tune. The only thing they constantly shared between them was the cloudy indigo-colored flame that came out from the pistil. Unlike the red flower, there did not seem to be any heat coming from them.

Jazmine tapped Davis's shoulder. "I think we need to get going. We don't want to accidentally run into this place's gardener."

"You're right. Let's just hope we can find the others quickly."

Davis led Jazmine to an entrance with no guards around it. Before walking through it, Jazmine used the camera on her phone to check what was inside by angling it around the corner. If anyone was waiting inside, she would know. Based on what she could see, the entrance led to an empty stone hallway that did not have any source of light.

"Which way do you want to go? Left, or right?" Jazmine asked.

"I think going to the right will be better. We'll more likely get into the castle's center that way."

"Yeah, typically in books, they have the prisons in the back or underground in the dungeon."

Jazmine took the lead in the search. She darted into the hallway and hugged the wall as she went further into it. Davis followed behind Jazmine, mimicking her movements. There was no clear indication of where they was going. The hallway had no windows, but Jazmine could see a light coming from the end of it on the left side.

If the fear of being caught by animal humanoids was not present, they would have loved exploring the castle. Even though they were indoors, nothing had changed from the outside. The hallway had moss coming from the cracks in the stone walls and grass poking out of the ground. Unlike Dalila's home, the people inside the castle allowed nature to run wild.

When they reached the end of the hallway, Jazmine pulled out her phone again to check what was behind the corner. The screen showed no one was there. Unlike the current hallway, this one had multiple doors leading down to a split. Jazmine looked back at Davis.

"There's a bunch of rooms down here. Do you think we should check in them as we walk past them?"

Davis shook his head. "We don't know what's on the other side of them. It's best if we move past them."

"Let's at least try to hear what's behind some of them."

Jazmine crept up to the first door in the hallway. The door was on the left-hand side and made of chestnut brown wood instead of stone; however, the doorknob was made of granite-like materials. Each door in the hallway had the same design.

Jazmine placed her ear on the door and tried to listen for what was on the other side. She could hear someone lightly snoring. Jazmine backed away from the door slowly and raised her finger to her mouth.

Jazmine mouthed, "Bedrooms."

Davis nodded.

They hurried down the hallway to check another room that was on the right side of the hallway. While she heard snoring like in the other room, it sounded different. She could hear to two distinct types of snoring. One sounded like a person, while the other, Jazmine assumed, was a snake.

"I think this whole hallway has bedrooms," Jazmine whispered.

"Then let's move on. We don't know if these are guards or regular workers," Davis said. "If we keep heading in one direction, then it will be easier for us to remember the way out of here."

"Then let's move towards the right. I think going left would take us to the front of the castle."

"Lead the way."

Jazmine turned into the new hallway. The doors were in a similar design to the ones that she passed. She pressed her ear onto a random door to hear what was on the other side. Once she heard snoring, Jazmine pointed down the hallway. Davis nodded as he understood nothing in this hallway would be helpful for them.

As they continued their way through the castle, Jazmine skipped the plain-looking doors. She assumed that once they got into the more essential sections of the castle, the doorways and hallways would be more decorative. They went down several hallways to see the difference that Jazmine thought would happen.

The difference between the hallway that they were currently in, and the past ones was immediate. Unlike the other hallways, there were paintings on the walls held up by golden snake frames. The paintings showed plant-like snakes in the trees, watching as Alorians were on the ground, trying to grow crops. The illustrations showed how the Alorians learned their magic.

Compared to the other doors they passed; someone made the doors in this hallway with higher-quality materials. Jazmine touched a door to see how it felt. It was smoother than the other ones. She did not know what type of wood it was, but it was darker and gave off a sweet scent. The doorknob looked like a purplish red well-polished Alexandrite.

"I know that half the planet is known for its minerals, but having a gem like this as a doorknob is baffling," Jazmine whispered.

The flooring of the hallway was better taken care of. The stone blocks were not cracked, but flowers were growing between them. Jazmine did not recognize one type of flower, as she did not find it in the castle's garden or the jungle.

There was one type of flower that looked like it was a mixture of metals and gems. The center of the flower had a gem that looked similar to a topaz with metal-like petals coming out of it. It was impossible for Jazmine not to recognize the other flower.

"Jazzy, isn't that the flower your family's crest is based on?"

"Yeah. Which means that either my adoptive dad is an Alorian or Ngo gave him the flower when he came here."

Davis tried to read Jazmine's face. He could not understand how she was feeling as her face remained blank. "Do you want to find a place where we can talk about it?"

"Nah, we should keep going and try to find the others."

"Alright."

He knew Jazmine would refuse to talk about it. Even if the question was bugging her, she would rather pretend it was not until she finished what was before her. Davis did not expect this conversation to come up again because the chance of Jazmine forgetting it was high. The only reason she talked about her problems with not accessing her magic and knowing that her guardians knew about said magic with Davis was because there was nothing to take her mind off it.

Jazmine looked at Davis. "Which door do you think I should check out next?"

"Well, I don't think there's a point in checking these doors anymore. If they locked everyone in a dungeon, I think it's better to find a place where the guards are."

"Then we should also be looking for anyone who looks like a scientist. We've been in this world for days, so they probably already started their experiments on them."

Chapter 26

Found

Jazmine and Davis found that getting through the castle was getting complicated. They were sure the sun had already risen because the castle workers were walking around. The Alorians in the castle did not always have their snake companions slithering next to them or wrapped around their bodies like in the village. Instead, it was like in the city where Alorians and snakes each had their own jobs to do.

Currently, Jazmine and Davis were hiding in a broom closet because a snake had turned the corner into their hallway. They left the door cracked so that they could see when the snake would slither through the hallway. The snake decided to slack off on its work today and coil itself up.

"Is it going to sleep?" Davis asked.

"It looks like it."

"What should we do now? We can't stay here all day."

"Let me try something."

Jazmine slowly opened the door to better examine the snake's position in the hallway. It had passed the broom closet, but with its enormous size, it made going around it complicated. The snake's head was not looking in her direction and instead was facing the open window located across the room. The area that they wanted to be was a little farther away from it. They would have to walk past the window if they wanted to get past the snake.

Davis peeked over Jazmine to see the snake as well. "What do you think?"

"Give me something to throw."

"I'm not about to let you hit the snake!" Davis snapped.

"I'm not trying to hit it," Jazmine explained. "I'm trying to see how deep it is sleeping. Then all we have to do is walk around it."

Davis looked at Jazmine before looking around to find something to give her. He found a small wooden floor scrubber. It was the perfect size to throw.

"Try this."

Jazmine took a step out of the closet with the scrubber in hand. Davis looked down the hallway in case someone was coming. He gave her a thumbs up. She nodded and chucked the scrubber toward the snake.

Thud.

Thankfully, it did not hit the snake, and it did not move from its spot. The impact was louder than Jazmine expected it to be. Even though they made it to the nicer side of the castle, it still lacked enough decorations to stop sounds from spreading. She was sure that the sound echoed in some of the other hallways.

Jazmine gave Davis a nervous smile. "At least it didn't wake up."

"Yeah, but we gotta get out of here before someone comes to check out what made that noise."

Sliding out of the closet, Davis brought out a broom and a mop with him. Jazmine gave him a confused look.

"What's that for?"

"We're in enemy territory," he explained, "so we're going to need something to protect us."

"Can I have the mop then?"

"Fine."

While Jazmine swung the mop around, Davis tried to step up over the snake. The animal was bigger when coiled up, so Davis had to hug the wall while stepping. He did not know if it was because he had overworked himself from running yesterday or if he did not get enough sleep but found it hard to get over the snake. The cloak that he was wearing did not make it any better.

"Jazzy, come on."

"Hold this," Jazmine said as she tossed her mop to Davis.

She took a few steps back and tied her cloak up to avoid it getting in her way. At full speed, Jazmine ran towards the snake before flipping over it. Without a hair out of place, she landed on her feet. Davis gave her a round of applause.

"It's a perfect score," he joked.

"I can't believe that being in gymnastics was helpful."

"Now we got to find a scenario where my soccer skills can shine."

Before they could continue joking around, the snake next to them sneezed. They jumped at how loud it was. It reminded them they had to get going before anyone found them.

As they continued through the castle, they found it harder to keep their cloaks on. They were too long, which caused it to drag on the ground. Davis had two close encounters because of it. He tried to tie his up like Jazmine did, but he had the same problem that she had, which was that the cloak had made her feel warm. They had to stuff them both in Jazmine's bag to move around comfortably.

"This is taking forever," Jazmine complained.

"Keep your voice down. Someone might hear us," Davis whispered.

"Davis, we have been in here for hours. If the guards or anyone in this place were good at their jobs, we would've been captured by now."

Davis gave Jazmine a horrified look. "You're right."

"The people in charge really need to fire everyone."

"No, Jazzy, you don't understand. You're right," Davis repeated. "These people had been watching us for who knows how long. Kidnapping one person would be easy, but getting three people, including Michael, shows they are competent enough to get us."

"You don't think they're messing with us, do you? What do they have to gain from doing this?"

A lot more than you know.

Looking around, Jazmine and Davis tried to find where the voice came from.

"Over here."

Jazmine and Davis turned to see the redheaded fox standing next to the tall werewolf. Being able to see their faces better, Jazmine thought that they looked young. The redhead looked like he could pass for their early twenties while the werewolf could pull off being a tall teenager.

"Found you," the werewolf said.

Davis leaned over to Jazmine. "What should we do?"

"I don't know, but she looks gorgeous."

The werewolf chuckled. He told the redhead something that got him mad.

"Just attack them already, Jadeite," the redheaded fox said. "And human, for your information, I'm a man."

Jadeite took off two rings that were on his thumb and middle fingers. He tossed the rings into the air. The rings morphed into metallic wolves with large pink petals and leaves peeking out from underneath their fur. The creatures were five feet tall and seemed to understand what was happening around them.

"Instead of me knocking their lights out, I'm gonna try out these bad boys," Jadeite said. "You have a problem with that, Silver?"

"Just make sure that they don't eat them."

Jadeite snapped his fingers. The wolves darted toward Jazmine and Davis. They barely had enough time to throw their weapons at the animated creatures. The wolves snapped the items with their jaws. Knowing they could not fight against the beasts; Davis grabbed Jazmine's hand and ran away.

"I love a chase," Jadeite said.

"They're getting away."

"Don't worry, I got their scents last night. There's nowhere they can run, too," he said before running off.

Jazmine and Davis darted through the halls. Since Silver and Jadeite had already found them, they did not care about trying to hide from the castle's residents. The Alorians and snakes either moved out of the way to let them pass or acted like nothing was happening. Unfortunately, Davis accidentally stepped on a snake's tail during their escape.

"Sorry!" Davis yelled.

"Does everyone in the castle know already?" Jazmine questioned.

Jazmine tried to use their freedom to her advantage. She pushed everything she could get her hands on to the ground to slow down Jadeite and his wolves. If Jazmine ran past someone holding something, she would slap it out of their hand.

The distractions did little against the wolves and Jadeite. The wolves jumped over any mess that was on the floor. Jadeite ran through everything. It did not matter if there was glass or food on the ground; he stepped on it as if it was nothing.

Jazmine did not understand how he did it since Jadeite wore no shoes. She was sure there had to be a few glass shards in his feet. It was like he had no feeling in his feet.

Davis noticed the pace at that Jadeite and his wolves were running. It didn't look like they were trying to catch them. None of them looked like they were out of breath like he was. Then an idea hit Davis. Jadeite was trying to tire them out.

"Jazzy, I don't think I can go on," Davis panted. "Too much is happening."

"Come on, Davis. There has to be a place where we can shake them."

"They were following us for who knows how long. We can't outrun them."

"Maybe we don't. Grab the cloaks out of my bag."

Davis slowed down so that he could unzip the backpack and get the cloaks. He did not know what Jazmine's plan was, but anything would be good at this point. Giving Jazmine a cloak, he watched as she sped up.

"Now, we gotta find a window to jump out of."

"Nope. Nope. We're not doing that."

Davis stopped mid-run. Stopping as well, Jazmine looked at him and then at the group chasing them. They stopped once, seeing that Davis had given up. Jadeite's tail wagged in amusement.

"This is gonna be good," he said to his wolves.

"What are you doing?"

"I rather die by whatever they plan to have instead of falling who knows how far down into the city."

"We'll be fine. Don't worry about it."

"Jazzy, this isn't a movie. We will die if we jump out of a window with only these cloaks."

"He's right, you know," Jadeite chimed in. "You need a cloak with Zephnia materials to float down safely."

"What's Zephnia?" Jazmine asked.

"Jazzy! Pay attention!"

"But it sounds like a nice place."

"It's alright. Pretty windy, but the whole landscape of the planet is made of mountains."

"Stop speaking to the enemy!"

Jadeite's wolves walked in front of Jazmine and Davis while they were talking. They did not know if they had to bite or subdue the humans, so they wanted until their master gave them a sign.

Jadeite, there's no reason you should explain anything if the rest aren't there.

Silver appeared next to Jadeite. Before anyone could move, Silver's eyes glowed a magenta color for a second. Jazmine and Davis felt themselves being lifted off the ground. They tilted forward as Silver walked away.

"Now, let's go. Your brother, Akaibara, is waiting for us along with the other humans."

"Yeah, yeah."

Signaling his wolves, Jadeite snapped his fingers. Jadeite's wolves looked at each other before launching themselves at Jadeite. They curled themselves up and shrunk down back to the size of a ring. Jadeite caught them and placed them back onto his fingers.

"Wait a minute, you're a telepath!" Jazmine yelled. She realized how Silver's actions made sense now.

Was talking directly into your mind not enough for you to figure out my powers?

"Can you read my mind right now?" Davis asked.

"Yes, you're thinking about the condition of your friends. There were some injuries within that group. After a few more weeks of recovery, the one named Michael should be fine."

"I forgot how fragile humans are," Jadeite commented.

"Wait! What's wrong with Michael? Is he okay?"

"As I just said, he will be healthy in a few weeks."

Davis could not think of how Michael could hurt himself badly enough that he needed weeks of recovery. Even when he was playing football, Michael was careful about his body.

Michael saw his body as the reason they accepted him into

school, as he barely passed the entrance test.

"Your thoughts are loud."

"I wonder why," Jazmine sang.

"Shut up."

***

As Jazmine floated through the halls, she took the time to admire

the castle, especially its paintings, since that was the only thing

she could see in her condition. There were differences in how

each was made. While some looked finger-painted, others were

made fine strokes to create them. Jazmine saw that whoever made

the painting signed their names at the bottom. She did not know if

the name was illegible because she did not know the language or

because of how horribly sloppy the person wrote it.

Due to Silver's telekinesis, Jazmine could not turn her

head to see what was in the rooms, but there were rooms with

large archways instead of doors. Jazmine could glance at what

was happening in the open space.

"Davis, the snakes are painting."

"Really? I can't see from this angle."

"Yeah, they're using their tails. They probably are the ones who created the paintings with the thinner strokes. What can you see on your side?"

"It's just windows that show the other parts of the tree."

"Whoever made this castle is dumb."

"That's what I've been saying. It makes sense to put the windows on the side facing the city," Jadeite said. A rose with a sharp point at the end of its stem flew at Jadeite. He caught it effortlessly and broke it in half. Akaibara walked out of the room. He crossed his arms as if he had heard what Jadeitie had said.

"Took you long enough."

"They ran off. I had to chase them. What do you want from me?"

"You could've outrun them in seconds. You just play around too much."

"Not my fault that I know how to have fun," he said. Jadeite shrugged his shoulders and pushed past Akaibara to get into the room. When he went in, someone peeked through the door. She might've a different hairstyle and outfit, but Jazmine and Davis could still tell who that was.

"Hua!" they yelled in union.

"Guys?"

Hua had styled her hair into one long braid that had five different flowers put into it. She wore a spaghetti lime green dress that reached just above her knees and a pair of beige sandals.

Silver dropped Jazmine and Davis to the ground. They ran at Hua and tackled her to the ground. When they did, Osmanthus slithered on top of Davis's head. Davis felt the new weight on his head and touched it to see what it was. After realizing it was a snake, he jumped off Hua, which caused Osmanthus to fall back on his partner.

"Why is a snake on me?"

"Don't worry, this is my partner, Osmanthus. Say hello, Osmanthus."

Osmanthus wiggled his tongue as a greeting.

"Hua? What's the commotion all about?" Ji-yoon asked as she walked towards the door. She had a different outfit as well. She'd found the chic equivalent of clothes in this world. Ji-yoon wore big, tan, wide-leg dress pants with a vine wrapped around her waist. Her olive-colored crop top showed the cuts she had gained through the jungle, but they seemed healed. Ji-yoon decided to keep her hair down, which was pushed back by a headband with a blue tourmaline in the center.

Rather than tackle Ji-yoon to the ground, Jazmine and Davis ran into the room to see their friend. They knew Ji-yoon would not let them jump on her as Hua did. Michael greeted them when they came in.

"Took you guys long enough." He could not get out of the chair that he was sitting in as a clay-like substance was wrapped around his left leg. The outfit given to him had less green in it than the others since the stylist used it as trimming to his shorts and crop top. He had his necklace wrapped around his wrist as a form of bracelet.

Davis could not take his eyes off Michael's abs.

You should close your mouth.

Davis did what he was told.

"Wait? Isn't Alex here?"

"She locked in our room," Ji-yoon explained. "She's been looking through all those journals she got from the butler."

"Oh."

Davis glanced at Jazmine. She did not change her facial expression after hearing that not only had her sister made it back to the mansion, but Ngo had given her the rest of the journals. It made no sense, and both knew it. Davis wondered when Jazmine would tell the others what they learned in the village. Since the things they learned revolved around her, Davis felt Jazmine should bring it up.

Before he turned his attention back to his other friends, Davis noticed Silver was watching him and Jazmine. Davis might not be able to read Jazmine's mind, but Silver could, which worried Davis. Silver's eyes connected with Davis. He gave Davis a smile before turning away.

"Why don't you all catch up while we fetch your friend?"

"Whatever you want. Hey Davis, come check out this view!" Michael called.

Hua grabbed Jazmine's hand. "And we can tell you want happened when we got split up. You would not believe what we went through."

The room that they were waiting in was beautiful. Sunlight came from the open window that overlooked the city and jungle. The plants inside this room appeared to be brought in instead of naturally grown, unlike other parts of the castle. Instead of paintings, emerald sculptures of snakes decorated the room.

Hua explained what she and the others had been through after being separated. Michael had to jump in occasionally to fill in the details his sister had missed. Davis explained the events that happened on his group journey. He tiptoed around Jazmine and Alexandra's argument because he did not know how much Alexandra had told them. He also kept the truth about Jazmine's parents to himself. If Jazmine wanted to talk about it, she would have done it.

No one realized how long they had been talking until their hosts came back into the room with Alexandra. She was wearing new clothing; however, it was things she owned. Now she wore a white button-up blouse with red trimming that had the top two buttons unfastened and a red plaid skirt. There was a vine wrapped around her waist like Ji-yoon, but it had a small grey pearl in the center. With her sleeves rolled up, everyone could see bandages wrapped around Alexandra's arms and hand.

It's time.

Chapter 27

Erased

Silver did not allow the group to react before teleporting them

somewhere in the castle. It was a secluded room at the back of the

castle. The enormous room had ten statues that touched the top of

the ceiling, placed in a circle facing in. An opened window the

width of the wall let fresh air into the room. The wind bothered

Silver enough to use his powers to put his hair into a ponytail.

The ones that did not know of his power were inquisitive about

how he could do that.

Jazmine was more focused on the obsidian statues that

were in the room. While she could not tell of what exactly,

Jazmine could see that most of the figures resembled animals.

She could see a snake and wolf sharing one podium together, and

on their left was a statue of a harpy, while a bear and phoenix shared another platform. A few podiums away, Jazmine saw a fox with multiple tails share a spot with a rabbit. Jazmine was sure these animals represented the world, but she could not tell what their magic was.

As Akaibara, Jadeite, and Silver stood together, the others were sitting down on flowers that Akaibara had created. It was soft but sturdy enough to hold each of their weights and did not seem to have any pollen.

"You two did better than your friends did," Jadeite laughed, breaking the ice. "The mess you made while running through the castle shows you're a Shadetorian descendant."

"What's a Shadetorian?" Hua asked.

"Oh yeah, it turns out that I'm not completely human," Jazmine said.

"I could've told you that," Alexandra mumbled.

"Guys, stay focused," Davis said. "What's going on here? Why did you bring us all here and not send us back through the portal?"

"Because you six are the keys that we needed to stop a pest that has been annoying us for quite some time. A person on your side has been stealing from our worlds."

"Namely, my half of the planet!" Akaibara yelled.

Michael turned to Jazmine and Alexandra. "Then that means...."

"The cure for cancer came from here," Jazmine finished.

"The Flower of Nature," Alexandra said. She leaned back in the flower and began tapping the petal where the armrest would be. Slowly, her hand went to her pocket. The vial that Ngo wanted her to give Jazmine was in her pocket. He probably made it with some plants found in the jungle.

"That species is too powerful for humans to have?" Akaibara asked. "Thankfully, only a small amount was taken because it is normally used to replace the plants destroyed by other magical actions."

"Cancer?" Jadeite asked, his ear perked up with confusion. He ignored what his brother had said. "What's that?"

"A human sickness," Silver answered. He scanned the faces of the teenagers. Jazmine and Davis knew what he was doing. Silver was reading their minds. While they did not like having their mind searched without permission, they knew they had no choice.

"So, how much are we supposed to tell them again?" Jadeite asked.

"We went over this," Akaibara scolded.

"First, greetings are necessary," Silver said. He placed a hand over his heart and bowed. "I am Silver, the crown prince of the Psynum people."

"As some of you know, I am the crown prince of the plant life Terrora, Akaibara. This is my younger twin brother." Akaibara nudged Jadeite to start his introduction. In that brief moment, his brother had already lost interest in the conversation.

"Jadeite. I rule over the earthy side of this world as crown prince."

Hua raised her hand. Akaibara was confused by her actions but pointed at her.

"I thought there could be only one crown prince to rule a nation or guess the world, in this case."

"For years, this the case," Silver said. "But due to the effects of the last group of humans that came into contact with our worlds and things of the past, things have changed."

"Things of the past?" Jazmine thought. Since she was sitting in the back, no one in her group could see her face. There was something that had already affected the world before her mother and her friends crossed the portal. Silver had continued talking without explaining what he meant by that. "He's hiding something."

"Are there any other questions before I get started?" Silver asked.

"Back in the ruins, I heard a voice," Hua said. "It was calling me. Do you know what that was?"

Akaibara and Jadeite gave each other a look that Jazmine almost did not see. Silver did not miss a beat with his response.

"There's nothing to worry about," he said with a smile.

Michael frowned at Silver's answer. He tried to stand up, but Davis held him down so his leg would not give out. "What do you mean, it's nothing to worry about? Whatever was calling her put her in some type of trace. If I didn't pull her out of the way, she would've fallen down the hole."

"But everything turned out fine, so there's nothing to worry about."

"You got to be kidding me," Michael scoffed.

"Prince Akaibara, do you know anything about it?" Ji-yoon asked.

"I said there is nothing to worry about."

Silver's eyes glowed magenta. The group felt a wave of pain go through their heads. Jazmine raised her hands to her head and tried to focus on something in the room to help her fight through whatever Silver was doing to them. She noticed that vines with purple flowers were inching closer to them.

"What are you doing to us?" Jazmine asked.

"Of course, I would affect you the least."

"Huh?"

While Jazmine's head hurt, it was not on the level of the others. Davis nearly fell out of his seat while Michael was bent over in pain. Alexandra almost lost consciousness. Jazmine heard Ji-yoon yell something in Korean. Osmanthus was trying to console Hua, who was crying, but even the snake looked like Silver's power had affected him. After a few minutes of torture, Silver's eyes stopped glowing.

"Now, do we have any questions before I start?"

"No sir," Hua said as she wiped the tears from her eyes.

"Yeah, we're all good," Michael added.

"Wait! What about that voice you heard in the ruins, Hua?" Jazmine asked.

"What voice?"

"We didn't see any ruins on our way here," Ji-yoon said.

Davis gave Jazmine a look. "You got to start paying attention when people tell you stuff."

Jazmine could not believe what she was hearing. She looked at Silver, whose expression did not change from the gentle smile. However, Akaibara and Jadeite's faces were more expressive. Akaibara refused to look any of them in the eyes, while Jadeite looked like he was holding back a laugh.

"Now that there aren't any more interruptions, Akaibara, will you help me with this?"

"Alright," Akaibara said as he snapped his fingers.

The flowers spat out a plum shade of fog that surrounded the group. Jazmine tried to swat the mist away, but the flower she was sitting on held her arms in place. She looked at Silver and saw that instead of his eyes glowing, it was his crown.

"Wait? Since when was he wearing a crown?"

It's best not to question my methods, especially if you want to learn about your parents.

Jazmine looked at Silver. The gentle smile he had turned into a smug one.

"We are called Royals," he said. "And this is our history."

Chapter 28

History Lesson

After breathing in the gas, Jazmine and the others found themselves floating miles above what looked like Terrora. Looking down, she could see how the world separated itself between jungle and desert. The jungle looked as lush as she saw it back on the cliff the first time, though now she could see the clearings better. The desert was vast but less empty than Jazmine thought it would be. Random rocks and metal popped out of the ground, and rocky plateaus were made of yellow sandstone.

"Is that the other part of the world?" Ji-yoon asked.

"I'm guessing so," Michael said. "That's the tree, and I guess that's the special place for people like Jadeite."

Michael pointed to a large, pointed object far off in the distance. It was hard for anyone to tell what it was from their position.

That is correct. This is Terrora, the land of the earth and plants. Home of the Alorians and Minedratils.

"Minedratils?" Davis repeated. "Is that what Jadeite is?"

Yes, I believe your people call his kind a werewolf or wolfman.

The group did not know if they were the ones moving or if the plant was rotating beneath them fast enough that it was possible to notice. They were moving away from the jungle and into the desert. Amazed, the plants that they could see in the desert were dead or areas of shrubs of grass with a single tree. Villages littered the area, but after inspecting the land, being nomadic was the lifestyle for some people.

"There are so many wolves," Ji-yoon said. Even from high above, it was easy for her to spot the unnaturally large wolves.

"Makes sense. Jadeite has wolf-like features similar to how Akaibara has snake features, and the jungle was full of those," Alexandra said.

There were craters carved into the ground, with some having caves they assumed had tunnels that led somewhere. They occasionally spotted canyons with some so deep that it was impossible to see the bottom of them. As they moved through the desert, the structure that Michael pointed out became bigger. It was the darkest shade of black they had ever seen and roughly the same size as the sacred tree. A castle and city were just a short distance from the structure. Instead of the castle being built to be large in length like in the tree, the Minedratils built their castle to be taller, but it still wide.

Terra is the largest of our planets. Within our realm, the people give up produce and raw materials that can be crafted. Your world benefits by being given nature, even though humans waste the gift by destroying it.

"Wait, so we're connected to this world more than through the portal?" Jazmine asked.

The portal is just a way for people who need help to cross over to do so themselves. However, the only portal left connected to your world is on this planet.

"What happened to the other portals on the other planets?" Davis asked.

The majority decided that you humans were too much of a pain to deal with physically. So, we Royals determined our faith in the comfort of our castles.

"What do you mean by deciding our faiths?" Alexandra asked. "Are the people here gods or something?"

Before explaining our job, you must know what we are and where we come from.

The group flew out of the atmosphere of Terrora and into space, where they could see seven planets in a circle with one in the middle. There was rock debris in between some worlds. Panic spread. The group thought they were going to die without air. Still, nothing happened. Michael pinched Alexandra to ensure the things happening were real. When she pinched him back, Michael pouted.

"You can't hit an injured person."

"Then don't pinch me. It hurts."

The plants that you see now are what's left of this universe.

"I'm guessing our plant is in another universe then," Davis said. "Wait, what do you mean? What's left of it?"

Unfortunately, not everything was peaceful in this universe. In fact, eons ago, the universe comprised one planet where all lived in harmony, but the history of what happened has been lost.

"Terrora is so big," Hua said.

"It's probably bigger than Jupiter," Alexander commented.

The planet on the right of Terrora is Pryas, the land of fire. The only reason humans learned how to make fire was because of them. The Dominos are some of the most loyal people you will ever meet.

Pryas had a few volcanoes that the group could see from space, but what surprised them was how much greenery they could see. They expected it to be like the earthy side of Terrora, where it was dry.

Following that is the planet of light, Solaria. It is home to the Hallees and Fairies, but I believe the Fairies immigrated to the land when their world was destroyed eons ago. The sun never sets on this planet.

"I want to visit there! I bet the fairies are cute," Hua said.

"They're probably different from the kinds you read in fairytales," Michael pointed out.

Jazmine shuddered when she looked at Solaria. The planet gave off a bright golden glow. It did not give off heat like Pryas, but Jazmine could tell the planet was very sunny. She did not know why, but the planet made her feel uncomfortable. Trying to find something to get her mind off Solaria, another planet caught her eye as she recognized it from her mother's journal.

"A planet of water and ice," she said. She pointed at a planet that was across from Terrora. From their distance, the planet looked blue and grey.

That is Hydros. Home to the Mermaids and Amphilerns, both races know their worth in the universe and will never settle for less. Thanks to them, your world has oceans, lakes, and rivers.

"Mermaids are real here?" Ji-yoon question. "I always wanted to be one."

"Are you serious?" Alexandra asked.

"What, you never had dreams like that?"

"My dreams are realistic."

"Stay focused," Davis scolded. "Silver, what is that planet between Solaria and Hydros?"

That is Protorics, the home of Trononics. Everything electric comes from them. Trononics have made great strides in technology and give humans the scraps of old prototypes made millenniums ago.

"How is that possible?" Alexandra asked. "People come up with their own things."

Usually, humans are given visions in the form of dreams to help them on their path. We let our people do things on their own most of the time.

"But why do we get the old stuff?" she mumbled.

"Protorics? Like in protons?" Davis wondered.

"That's cute," Ji-yoon said.

Protorics did not have colors that defined the planet like the others did because it was hard to look at due to the flashing lights that inhabitants were using. They could tell how much electricity played a part in their world. If they had a hand in making the things in their world, their land had to be advanced.

After Hydros, it is Zephnia, the land of wind and air. The people of this world are equivalent to creatures like' harpies in your world, but they are actually called Zephees. My good friend

rules over this world.

The group could see that mountain ranges completely covered the planet. The thick fog made it impossible to tell what else was on the planet.

"That's the place Jadeite mentioned," Davis said. "He said it would be possible for us to fly with material from their world."

"The planet is probably windy," Hua said. "I will put my hair up if we go there."

We call the last of the creator worlds Shadtulus, the land of darkness and magic. The Shadetorians give thanks to the moon, stars, and everything else the universe offers. The only thing that can stop a Shadetorian is their creativity.

"That's where I descend from?"

Jazmine looked down at the planet. She noticed it gave off a better aura than Solaria. The planet was dark purple and had nothing else that stood out like the other planets, yet the beauty of it still amazed her.

Davis gave Jazmine a friendly elbow to her side. "It makes sense about your creativity. You could create something great if you had more drive to do something."

"Your magic is limitless," Alexandra whispered. She touched her pocket, holding the liquid Ngo gave her for Jazmine. Alexandra grimaced. "Of course, your magic is limitless."

"Can you zoom in like you did in Terrora?" Jazmine asked. "I want to see what it looks like."

Sorry, I was told not to.

"Told not to? By whom?"

Carrying on, there are other types of magic whose world they have lost. Fairies are skilled in magic relating to hope, but they are so rare I only know the ones who are Royals. My race is Psynum, and, as you all should know, my people use magic that shapes the mind.

The planet of Niji has been lost for centuries now, but luckily it was common for their race to move to their spouse's world, so not all of them are gone. Given the same name as their lost planet, Niji uses the magic of the heart.

The odd ones out are the ones who possess soul-magic capabilities. It has never been documented or passed down any mention that they had their own planet. In fact, only a handful are

born randomly every few years. Those who have such power are

called Vitalnomus.

"Wait! You haven't answered me yet!" Jazmine yelled.

But as you all can see, there is another planet. Our

ancestors recently created the planet in the middle within the last

millennium.

"Don't ignore me!"

Quiet, I'm talking. Our ancestors created this nameless

world for races that do not have a planet anymore like mine to

live on. Other races that have their planets may still live here.

Because this world has multiple races, it is typical for people to

gain access to numerous types of magic. However, a person will

always have one main magic they excel at. Because of the planet

being a sign of peace and new beginnings, it was later given the

name Magix.

"How creative," Jazmine mocked.

You had a stuffed animal that you named Dog because it

was a dog. For a Shadetorian descent, you should be ashamed of

yourself.

"Listen, names are hard for me."

Then keep your comments to yourself. Before the creation of Magix, the ancestors had to practice their skills to create the utopia that is Magix. This is how your universe came to be. The lives that are in your solar system were handcrafted and studied to find any problems that might arise in Magix.

"So, humanity was just their guinea pig?" Ji-yoon asked.

And the beings on other planets. I'm going to focus on Earth because it has become a popular show to watch.

"They treat our lives like it's television," Ji-yoon realized.

"I have a question. Elder Dalila told Jazmine and me that humans have access to magic, but it is rare for them to activate it. Did the ancestors give us magic?" Davis asked.

I do not know. It is a strange phenomenon that humans have magic.

"For all we know, we could be mixed with different things," Davis said.

"I must excel in plant magic. And Alexandra's is fire," Hua said. "Those are the only things we have been able to do."

Jazmine looked at her sister. "Is that why you have bandages on your arm?"

"It's specially made so that I won't combust randomly."

Reaching her out, Jazmine tried to touch her sister's arm. Alexandra yanked it away before Jazmine could feel it. Jazmine gave her a worried look.

"Does it hurt?"

"I'm fine."

Jazmine nodded. She turned her attention back to the planets, but she could feel the eyes of the others on her and Alexandra.

Michael was about to say something, but Davis covered his mouth. He glared at Alexandra, who was fiddling with her pockets. Hua patted her brother's back with a sigh to calm down. Ji-yoon looked between Jazmine and Alexandra before looking down.

May I get back to my explanation?

"Please do!" Hua yelled.

Each world, past and present, has a magical element that helps balance the universe. Each element bestows specific individuals' power that is enough to destroy planets or cause disasters around them or even on your planet. The things that you call natural disasters aren't natural.

The ones with this tremendous power are called Royals.
Elements can pick who the next Royal is when that person shows
an excellent understanding of that element. Still, it can be genetic.
I am good friends with the queen of Hydros, and she is the Royal
of Water. Her grandfather was a Royal of Water. The daughter is
one of the Royals of Darkness. While her great-grandfather is the
Royal of Earth and Plant Life, and her great-grandmother is a
Royal of Light. These two are some of the strongest beings that
exist.

"So why does the great granddad have two elements, but it's separated between siblings like Akaibara and Jadeite?" Davis asked.

Those two elements were always meant to be separate.
One who can use plant magic cannot use any other type of magic,
yet he could. The elements must've blessed him at birth.

"That means I will be only able to use plant magic."

Osmanthus rubbed his face against Hua. He whispered something in her ear that made her laugh. She hoped she could use multiple types of magic, but having Osmanthus was a good substitute.

"You said something earlier about us helping take care of a pest. What happens if we refuse?" Alexandra asked.

"Lex!"

"What? Just because a human is causing trouble does not mean we have to be the ones dealing with it. If you Royals are so strong, then why isn't one of you doing something?"

We could, but we found this is better. You, Hua, and Davis will not be permitted back onto Earth even if you do not fulfill this task.

"What do you mean the three of us can't go back?" Hua asked.

"Yeah, we have families to return to," Davis added.

The three of you have unlocked your magic. While at different degrees, if you go back to your planet, you would be a danger to yourself and others.

Alexandra grabbed her arms while Hua thought about what could happen if she tried to touch the plants that were in the school. They found the situation understandable. Davis was the only one who could not understand Silver's logic.

"But I haven't done any magic yet!"

"Yeah, I was with him the entire time and never noticed anything."

Did you not feel that someone was watching you?

"Well, yeah, but-"

No one else could do that. You found the area where Akaibara's spy was because you sensed his soul inside a snake he created. You have a rare magic inside of you.

"Soul magic," Davis repeated.

My time is up for this lecture.

The group felt lightheaded. Everything around them started to be replaced with a plum shade of fog. They slowly lost sight of each other. Silver's voice could no longer be in their heads.

When the fog cleared from the room, the group regained consciousness. Jazmine saw that Jadeite was wearing a strange mask that covered his nose and mouth. She guessed that the smoke would have some type of effect on him. If Jadeite was holding back in catching her and Davis, then Jazmine assumed that Jadeite had the same characteristics as a wolf. He could not handle the smell.

"While resting, we will discuss with our equals how you will help us," Silver said.

"I already made another bedroom available for your group to use," Akaibara said.

"Yeah, and some of you need to bathe," Jadeite said.

"Funny how the one who rolls around in the dirt says that."

Before Jadeite could argue back, Silver placed his hand over the brothers' mouths. He gave the group a smile.

"Have a nice rest of your day."

Chapter 29

Letting It Out

After explaining this world and the others, the Royals allowed Jazmine and her friends to explore the castle to their hearts' desire. Davis had helped Michael return to the room he was sharing with his sister. Michael wanted to milk his injury to the fullest with Davis, even though Hua had complained that he hadn't let anyone help him recover before.

"Well, that was before I had a cute nurse," Michael replied when asked about it. Davis gently punched him in the shoulder but said nothing about the statement. Jazmine was sure that she saw him smile when he turned his head.

Hua had left with Osmanthus to train. She had begun a short internship with the housekeepers to help her control her newly awakened powers. Ji-yoon had gone with her to learn what was happening within the castle. There was still a language barrier, but she felt it would be fine. Ji-yoon said that she could figure out what they were saying by body expressions, and if she needed to, Hua would translate what the snakes said.

Jazmine planned to bathe before napping under the sun, but her sister stopped her before she could do so. Alexandra pushed Jazmine into the room that she was sharing with Ji-yoon.

"What's the big idea?"

"Shut up and come in."

Jazmine could tell which side of the room was her sister's. While Ji-yoon's side was tidy, Alexandra made her side of the room look exactly like her room back in the mansion. Journals littered her side. Jazmine could not understand how her sister could treat books like this.

When asked how she got the journals, Alexandra explained what had happened when she returned to their world. She did not tell the others what had happened to her because she felt it was not their business to know. Jazmine would be the only person to understand the severity of the problem.

"Jazmine, look. All of them are blank."

Jazmine walked up to the journals that Alexandra had spread out on the floor. Just as she said, the books were blank. Jazmine double-checked the journals she had read, but not even the pictures were safe. The photo slots were empty, and the drawings looked like they had been erased.

"How is this possible? I've read some of them, and they definitely had things written in them. Wait, let me check the one I have."

Jazmine pulled out the journal that she had in her bag. Flipping through the pages, whatever had happened to the journals that Alexandra had now affected the one that Jazmine had. The only thing that was not affected was the photo of her mother and friends. She wondered if Silver had something to do with this, but it seemed impossible. Silver could erase people's memories, but changing physical things appeared to be out of his reach.

"And when did this happen? I looked through the journal on this planet a few days ago."

"Well, these were blank the minute I looked at them. The same day, Akaibara took me and the others to the castle. From what Ji-yoon said, an entire day had passed in this world."

"Freaky. Do you think another Royal is trying to give us a test or something? Silver and the others said that we're going through a task or something to ensure that we are safe to be in this universe."

"Well, whoever it was only allowed us to keep the picture."

"That's fine by me. This is the only picture I have of my mom."

"Excuse me? Your mom is in that picture?" Alexandra questioned. Alexandra's eyes widened at the news. The way Jazmine had said it causally caught Alexandra off guard. Jadeite did mention earlier how Jazmine was a Shadetorian descendent, but Alexandra did not expect this.

Jazmine shrugged her shoulders nonchalantly. "Well, the village elder Davis and I met knew who my parents were and could pick out my mom from the picture. I think my father was the person who took the photo since everyone here looks human."

"Maybe one of your parents isn't of direct blood, either. Maybe your mom was the one you get your Shadetorian blood from?"

"From what Dalila told me, my dad was a Shadetorian. And before it went blank, the journal confirmed it because my mom kept mentioning how a person knew of this place. And there were pictures of a guy blocking the camera, so his face was never seen."

"I can't believe it." Alexandra pushed some journals off the bed so that she could sit down. She had to process what Jazmine had said. While she was coming to terms with everything, Jazmine picked up the books from the ground.

"Just because the journals are blank doesn't mean you should mistreat them."

"Do you not realize how big this is, Jazmine? You have an idea of who your parents are!"

"Oh, I understand. I understand that my whole life, the people taking care of me have kept secrets about my ancestry. I understand I could've known so much more about my mother if it wasn't for someone erasing the journals," Jazmine said as she slammed the journals on top of each other. "And I understand that there's a possibility that both are them are...."

Jazmine could not finish her sentence. It was too painful for her to think about it, but Alexandra understood. The two of them were always told that their parents had died in some sort of accident together. Yet, everything was different now.

If someone was trying to stop Jazmine from learning about her mother and her adventures, then her parents could be alive. Alexandra believed that this hurt Jazmine the most. The possibility that they were alive would mean coming to terms with the fact that they decided not to be in her life for whatever reason.

"Wait, who are *my* parents, and what happened to them?"

"What do you mean?"

"If Dad, or rather Steven and Ngo, had always said that our parents died together, and if there is a possibility that your parents aren't actually dead, then what happened to mine?"

"I don't know. Do you think your parents are in this picture? Maybe we can ask one of the Royals if they've seen them before," Jazmine said. She did not want to ask for their help, least of all Silver's. The others still believed he was safe to be around, and she had no proof to say otherwise. Until she had evidence, Jazmine was going with the flow.

Alexandra shook her head. "Asking them would be a waste. You said an elder knew your parents. Those guys are too young to have met them."

"I guess you're right."

Jazmine fiddled with her fingers. She opened her mouth to say something but quickly closed it. Alexandra overlooked her sister's actions as she was too busy fixing her hair.

"Hey, Alex."

"What?"

"You're not mad about what happened a few days ago, right? Because I really thought moving forward at that moment would have to be better."

"It's fine," Alexandra said without looking away from her mirror.

"Are you sure?"

"It's fine."

"Alright. I'm going to take a bath if you need anything. Love you."

Jazmine stood still for a moment before leaving the room. Alexandra watched through her mirror as Jazmine walked out. When she stopped hearing Jazmine's footsteps, Alexandra placed the mirror on the night table. Pulling out the small bottle she was supposed to give to Jazmine, Alexandra grinned.

"It's fine alright. I'm fine enough to make sure that you won't be able to fully connect with your parents. How sad that a person in the direct descent of magical beings can't use magic," Alexandra giggled.

Chapter 30

Understanding

After having an eventful day, Jazmine tried her best to relax. The housekeepers that had given her new clothes were handstitched to have elements of Shadetorian customs. While they had limited colors on hand, Jazmine's clothing comprised of a Tyrian purple sleeveless top with black shorts that came down to her knees. Jazmine left her shoes back in her room to explore the castle barefoot.

"Days must be long here because I'm sure my nap lasted over an hour," Jazmine thought.

She yawned as she walked through the hallways. Jazmine had forgotten how to get back to her room, and she couldn't recognize anyone that she was passing. She believed if she kept walking, she would find someone. Within forty-five minutes,

334

Jazmine finally heard a voice that she recognized. Unfortunately, it was Silver's voice. Jazmine peeked into the room that he was in. She realized it was the room with the statutes that she was in earlier.

Although it was hard to see, Jazmine could tell that Silver was not talking to anyone physically. Instead, there was a small purple orb he was looking into.

"Did you notice anything special about her?" a feminine voice asked.

"That's the odd thing. Her powers feel as if something has made it harder for her to awaken it."

"Is it a spell? I can try to reverse it if it is."

"No, not a spell. And there is a cure for it, but I want to see if the other one will give it to her."

Jazmine tried to lean in closer to better hear what Silver was talking about. She did not understand the conversation, but it was clear it was about her or one of the others.

"Ji-yoon and I are the only girls left who haven't had their magic unlocked," she thought. "I wonder which one he's talking about."

Did you need something?

Jazmine jumped at the sudden voice in her mind. She fell into the room. Looking up, she saw Silver looking at her with a blank face. The orb he was talking to lost its purple color and was now a clear crystal ball.

"Well, you know, just hanging around. Smelling the flowers. All that stuff."

You remind me a lot of my friend. She can't lie on the spot, either.

Jazmine laughed. She walked over to Silver, who motioned his orb to disappear. He pushed his bangs out of his face and smiled.

"So, who were you talking to?"

"A fellow Royal."

"A Royal of what?"

"You will figure it out in due time."

Jazmine huffed. She turned towards the statues, which she now had a better view of. Starting from the podium with the snake and wolf, she looked around each one carefully. There was a phoenix with a bear on one platform, but there were creatures with their own podium, such as a harpy, a Pegasus, and more. The one that caught Jazmine's eye was the statue of a dragon.

"I know some of these. Does that mean that these are—"

"Yes, these are the protectors of our elements. As you know, the wolf and snake represent the earth and plant life."

Jazmine pointed at the podium, holding a fox and a hare. "I know the fox is psychic abilities, but what about the bunny?"

"That's a hare, and it represents the same as the fox."

"How's that possible?"

"Just because you see two creatures does not mean it will have two elements, like in Protonic, there is a monkey and a cat. Two different animals, but they still have the element of electricity. The magic found on this planet can be compared to a sword and shield, which can also be seen in the princes."

"What do you mean?"

"Jadeite is more hotheaded than you have seen. He would have accidentally hurt you or your friend during the chase if not for his medicine. On the other hand, Akaibara is the levelheaded one that gets riled up occasionally. Jadeite excels with attacking, while Akaibara will block any attack that comes his brother's way."

Jazmine thought over what Silver said. From what she saw of Jadeite, he seemed more active than Akaibara. Her mind

337

wondered about other things. If they had a definitive fighting style, the other Royals and their elements must have their own. She looked back at the statues to guess how they would act in a fight. Jazmine looked at the podium that had the fox and hare on it.

"I wonder what he would look like with bunny ears," Jazmine thought.

Silver chuckled before closing his eyes. His tail shrunk into his clothing, and a pair of hairy ears appeared. The newly formed ears were just as red as his hair. When finished, Silver gave Jazmine a sheepish smile.

"I rarely show my ears to anyone I just meet."

"How did you do that?"

"Being a Royal, I can change between the two at will."

"Cool."

Jazmine fiddled with the end of her shirt. Without peeking into her mind, Silver could tell that Jazmine wanted to ask him something. He sighed.

"Do you want to feel my ears?"

"Yes! But I also wanted to know what you did to my friends when they asked you about the voice that Hua heard."

Silver sighed again. He looked over at the statue of the dragon. "While the creatures of the elements rather stay on their own planet except for being on Earth, dragons are unpredictable, just like the ones over them."

Jazmine's eyes sparkled. "There's a dragon here?"

"Two, to be exact. One for each part of the planet. I don't know why it called out to your friend when she can't free it, but I could not risk them wanting to return to the ruins to find it."

"How can the dragon be freed then?"

"The only way someone can free a dragon is by being a Royal of Darkness or having a connection to dragons."

"Maybe Hua has a connection to dragons she doesn't know about?"

"Or maybe she is friends with someone related to someone with a connection to dragons?" Silver rebutted. "The one calling out to your friend probably got confused by her scent."

Jazmine thought about what Silver was telling her. She wanted to tell the others their minds had been wiped, but she was glad she did not. Besides him warning her that the others learning about dragons could be dangerous, Jazmine had the feeling that

339

they were nowhere near ready to face something like that. They nearly died from the animals and plants native to this planet.

She looked at the dragon statue. Silver could tell how much was weighing on the girl, even if she did not vocalize it. He gently placed his hand on top of Jazmine's head. She gave him a weak smile in return.

"You know, I think it's amazing I'm learning more about myself, but it scary," Jazmine said. "And it's not just me who's changing."

"You and your friends were bound to grow in change no matter what," Silver explained. "I find that, being here, the words will show what type of people you six are."

Jazmine nodded in agreement.

"Can I touch your ears now?"

"Go ahead." Silver sighed.

Chapter 31

First Task

It had been three weeks since the group learned about the
elements and everything else about the planets in this universe.
During the three weeks, Jadeite mentioned how a decision was
already made for the group's tasks. Akaibara and Silver wanted to
tell them after Michael was fully recovered, as they warned the
tasks would be laborious for them.

To be ready for the tasks, Hua and Davis did their best to
try to control their magic. Hua had better results than Davis, as
she could learn from the housekeepers. Thanks to Silver's magic,
Hua and the rest of the group had a better understanding of the
local language. None of them were fluent, but they could hold
small conversations. She tried to practice with the guards, but
their level of magic was too advanced for her. Akaibara had to

341

explain that she could not do half of what the guards had been doing for a long time.

Davis did not have the luxury of watching anyone with his magic. No one in the castle had that type of magic that he could learn from. However, Silver told him that even if someone was there, he could not learn from them. Soul magic users had their own way of controlling their powers. What Davis manifested with his magic would be his creation, so he was given a bracelet with an Aventurine to remind him of it. The rest of the outfit was a pair of brown shorts and a teal sleeveless shirt.

Alexandra was told she could not practice her magic because she was in a highly flammable environment. It did not bother her, as she had no interest in training. She was more focused on trying to uncover the magic that was in the journals. Alexandra could be found in the castle's library if she was not in her room. Whenever someone tried to talk to her, she would brush them off. Only Ji-yoon could hold a conversation with her.

The group was told to wait in the room with the statues until Akaibara and Silver arrived. Jadeite had left two weeks previously. He did not mention why, but Akaibara told them it was nothing to worry about. While they wanted their hosts, the group divided themselves into two smaller groups. Alexandra and Ji-yoon paired up, and the others stayed together.

"Did I do something to make her mad?" Hua asked her brother.

"No, she's just inherently mean."

Alexandra heard Michael's comment and gave him a look before continuing her conversation with Ji-yoon. Michael raised a finger at her, but Hua and Davis quickly grabbed his hand. Hua scolded him for being mean to her, while Davis told him he should be more mature. While Alexandra did not see it, Ji-yoon did and laughed. She lied to Alexandra by saying that she remembered something funny.

Silver and Akaibara walked into the room after ten minutes. Akaibara's snake was not in his staff form but wrapped around Akaibara's body. Even though Akaibara did not look physically as strong as his brother, it was impressive that he could carry a snake that large.

Michael shivered at the sight of his snake. While he had grown used to seeing diverse types of snakes during his stay, he still did not like being around them. It was hard for Hua to get him anywhere near her when Osmanthus was on her. Michael could swear that he could hear Alexandra snickering at his reaction.

"Good to see you all today," Silver greeted.

"Sorry it took so long," Akaibara apologized. "We got caught up with something."

Davis shook Jazmine, who was sitting next to him, awake. She had fallen asleep as she was the first person who made it. The others had entered the room fifteen minutes ago, but Jazmine came in an hour before them because she accidentally found her way into the room. She was sure that if she left, she would not find the room again.

The group had gotten to their feet. They were curious to know if the task would be physical or if it would be a mental task. Hua and Davis were the only ones who looked nervous, as the others' emotions ranged from boredom to curiosity.

When she got up, Jazmine tucked a book with her name on it into her bag. No one had questioned her about what she was doing with the book, but she had noticed that she had gotten it within the first week of staying in the castle.

Silver snapped his fingers. A red and black cell phone appeared. It was in a unique style that the group had seen, but

344

there were some similarities to their phones. Silver's phone was a touchscreen and had childish stickers stuck on his phone case. No one recognized the characters but knew it was from some type of cartoon.

"Wait, if you had a phone, why did I see you use a crystal ball earlier?"

"Because it was easier for you to overhear if I use that instead of my phone."

Jazmine was speechless. There was no way that Silver could have guessed that she would accidentally make it to the room he was in. Even if he had psychic powers, he would have to have the ability to see into the future, which seemed farfetched to Jazmine.

Tapping through his phone, Silver pulled up a holographic 3D model of the castle that Jadeite lived in and the surrounding area. It was big enough for everyone to see but it did not crowd the room.

Amazed at the technology, Ji-yoon took a step forward toward the hologram. She reached out to touch it, but her hand went through the image. It was in full color and could be mistaken for a diorama by how realistic it looked. The hologram looked precisely how the group saw it in the fog.

"This will be your first task," Silver said. "You must make it to the castles on each planet, with the first being the castle in the earth kingdom. Unlike your time through the forest, there will be no one helping you."

"And we won't be watching you either," Akaibara added.

Hua raised her hand. "But what happens if we get into a dangerous situation?"

"Some of you already have unlocked your magic, so everything should be fine," Silver said.

"Or, in the words of my brother, you die."

Hua did not feel confident about their answer. She began pulling on her dress until Ji-yoon grabbed her hand. Squeezing Hua's hand, Ji-yoon gave her a smile. Ji-yoon was not confident either, but she did not want Hua to worry.

Michael clicked his tongue. "What about wild animals? The snakes here nearly ate us."

"Oh, the snakes here are herbivores, so they weren't going to eat you," Akaibara explained. "They were just angry that you were in their territory."

"So that's why Osmanthus only eats leaves," Hua whispered.

"But what about the wolves? Aren't those common on that side of the planet?" Michael asked. "I'm guessing that they aren't herbivores."

"Just don't run into them."

It took everything that Michael had in him to not hit Akaibara.

"Overall, the task should be easy for all of you," Silver said. "I recommend leaving in—"

"You said that this is the first task," Alexandra interrupted. "What about the other tasks? You and your acquaintance had weeks to figure out what we should do to help even though we never got a choice."

"Lex, don't be rude," Ji-yoon hushed.

"I'm not being rude. He's not telling us the whole thing."

Jazmine looked at her sister before turning to Silver and Akaibara. She could tell that Alexandra was disgusted with Akaibara. He did not try to hide his facial expression. His nose was drawn up and wrinkled as if he smelled something terrible.

Even if he could hide his face, Akaibara's snake hissed at Alexandra to show his displeasure.

Silver tried to keep his face straight, but Jazmine could tell that he was getting annoyed. Placing his phone back into his pocket, Silver wanted to explain himself.

"Well, I'm telling you what we agreed on. All of you will go to the castles to meet the Royals who oversee their planet. Whatever their tasks are is something that they only know."

"What? You didn't feel like reading their minds?"

"Alex!" Hua yelled.

Alexandra ignored Hua. She crossed her arms and gave Silver a condescending look. After taking a deep breath, Silver smiled.

"I don't read my friends' minds. Plus, people are allowed to keep their secrets. I know that you have plenty of those," Silver said. He casually put his hands in his pockets and began to play with his phone that was in it. Alexandra narrowed her eyes but stayed quiet.

"To finish what Silver was saying," Akaibara started, "we believe you all should start your journey within a few days. We will give you supplies, so there is no reason for you to worry about that."

"Thanks, we appreciate it," Jazmine said.

"Let us talk this over before we give you a certain day," Davis added.

"Of course, take as long as you need."

***

Everyone was currently sitting in a circle in the castle's garden. After being told what their first task was, it divided the group about what to do. Everyone had their reasons for whether they should do the task or not.

Alexandra thought that doing the tasks was a bad idea. She would rather go back home and pretend that none of this had happened. Even though Ngo told her not to come back, she found his lack of reasoning enough for her ignore him. Alexandra never told Jazmine or the others what Ngo said to her, and she planned to keep it like that.

Jazmine thought that doing the task was a fantastic idea. She believed this would bring her closer to her biological parents. Confused why Alexandra did not want to do it; this would have been a fantastic way to find out more about her parents as well.

Jazmine also thought that this would be a once-in-a-lifetime opportunity for everyone.

Hua did not like the idea of going. She feared something terrible would happen to someone, which would be her fault. Hua was the strongest in the group because of her magic, so she would have to save the day if something happened.

"I couldn't save Alexandra from the rose monster," she thought. Hua tugged at the end of her dress to help her calm down. She looked over at her big brother.

Michael was okay with going on the journey. Even though he was recently recovered from an injury, Michael thought it would be interesting to complete the task. The only problem that he had was that Hua had the chance of getting hurt. When he voiced his concern, Hua claimed she could take care of herself. She mentally facepalmed when she did. Now, it looked like she wanted to go.

Davis tried to be the mediator, but Alexandra said he could not because he wanted to complete the task. He tried to explain that it did not matter. No one should argue with each other.

Ji-yoon was the only person who did not voice her opinion, as she was too busy going through her phone.

"Alexandra, we don't know how to control our powers, so we can't go back even if we wanted to," Davis explained.

"I'll be fine if I have these bandages on. Plus, it's not like your magic has done anything destructive."

"That's not the point."

"There's no point in arguing with her," Michael said. "She's too selfish to think of anyone but herself."

"Excuse you!"

"Come on, guys, don't fight," Hua said. "We're all friends here."

"We aren't friends," Alexandra and Michael said together.

"Why don't we hold a vote?" Ji-yoon questioned. "The majority is what we will go with."

"No!" Alexandra yelled. "That's how we got into this in the first place!"

"And I remember you lost that too," Michael laughed.

Alexandra raised her hand to hit Michael, but Ji-yoon forced her hand down. Alexandra gave her friend a look, but it did nothing to Ji-yoon.

"What's your position in this, anyway?" Alexandra asked.

"If it keeps me away from my family, then I'm fine with going."

"I didn't even think about that," Michael said. "I'm definitely going now."

"Michael," Hua said.

"What? It's not like I was returning home for the holidays."

"Ngo will be fine by himself," Jazmine said. "Plus, he would understand since he came here before."

Alexandra looked around to find someone that she could turn to her side. Hua was an option, but Michael would shut anything she said down. Then her attention turned towards Davis. Even with his fear of losing control of his magic, Alexandra knew what to say to get him to waver.

"Davis, are you really going to leave your poor mother behind?" Alexandra asked. "Out of everyone, you're closest to your parent."

"I..."

Davis looked down at his hands. He fidgeted with his fingers as he thought about what he wanted to say. Of course, he did not want to leave his mother for an undetermined amount of time, but he knew he would have to.

Michael put his hand on Davis's shoulder. "That's not far for you to ask that."

"Yeah, you can't say that," Jazmine agreed. "It's like you're forcing him into something he doesn't want to do."

"I would never do that. I just wanted him to know the consequences of him staying here."

Michael was about to say something, but Davis beat him to the punch.

"Thank you for worrying about me, Alexandra, but I still believe it is in everyone's best interest that we complete the task given to us."

Alexandra tried her best to hide her anger. There was nothing she could do to get her way. After a moment, she nodded begrudgingly.

"Fine. If you all want to go, I guess that I'll go too."

Jazmine clapped her hands together. "See, everything worked out."

"I'll tell Prince Akaibara and Silver the news. I think three days should be enough time for us to get ready," Ji-yoon said as she got up.

Jazmine sat back against a wall as everyone got up to leave. When everyone was gone, she pulled out the book with her name on it from her bag. She flipped through a few pages before beginning to write in it.

December XX

Everyone agreed on going on the journey to the different castles, well, except for Alex. She's still going, though. I don't know what I'm going to see, but I know I will eventually find you and Dad. And when I do, I will be able to use the coolest magic you have ever seen.

Talk to you later, Mom.

~Jazmine Lee~

Epilogue

It had been approximately four days since the group had left the castle. With their first task being finding their way to Jadeite's kingdom, the group was unsure when they would make it. The landscape was worse than the jungle. Even with the supplies given to them, they found it difficult to agree on how to get there.

"We should keep heading northwest!" Alexandra yelled. "It is a direct line to the other castle!"

"But the map said that we should head northeast because that path will lead us around the canyon," Michael pointed out. "Your way would make us have to climb down, find a way across the river, and climb back up the canyon. And I, for one, refuse to do that."

"We'll be out here for weeks with your plan, Michael. And they did not give us enough food to be in the desert for that long!"

"Well, with yours plans, we'll be out here for months!"

"Stop trying to one-up me!"

"Come on, guys, let's not fight," Hua chimed.

"There's no stopping those two," Ji-yoon stated.

"But-"

"Give it up, kid," Ji-yoon said as she placed her hand on Hua's shoulder. Hua mumbled something about not being a kid under her breath, which caused Osmanthus to rub his head against hers.

Jazmine and Davis watched as their friends argued with each other. This was Alexandra and Michael's fifth fight today. It was at a point where Davis was tired of trying to break them up. Jazmine had to remind him that they would eventually wear themselves out. However, Davis stayed in the back in case someone wanted to leave out of anger. Jazmine was in the back because she was focused on writing in the journal.

Suddenly, Davis looked up at one of the rocky columns to his left. For a split second, he could have sworn he saw two figures on top of a column, but when he blinked, they were gone.

"What's wrong?" Jazmine asked.

"I thought I saw something. Must've been my imagination," Davis said as he shook his head. "Come on, the others are getting ahead of us."

Jazmine looked at the rock column that Davis was looking at. Nothing seemed out of the ordinary to her. She shrugged her shoulders before running to catch up with the others. It did not matter if Davis saw something because what was the worst that could happen when they were all together?

"It's probably Silver and someone else," she thought.

Acknowledgments

This book took me a few years to complete, and I had people cheering me on throughout that time. First, I would like to thank my mom, who always encouraged my writing even though she is not a reader. She had understood little of how I was doing this, but she still supported me. Next, I want to thank my dad. He had always wanted me to use my brain for work instead of doing anything physical. I cannot forget to thank my brothers, sisters, and sister-in-law. Lastly, I would like to thank the remainder of my family and friends who knew about me working on a book that cheered me on.

www.ingramcontent.com/pod-product-compliance
Lightning Source LLC
Chambersburg PA
CBHW010829250626
47157CB00010B/3220